EIGHT BALL IN THE SAND TRAP

NASH RUNNING BEAR MYSTERY
BOOK EIGHT

BAER CHARLTON

Cover design by Roslyn McFarland, Far Lands Publishing

Sketch artist Kelly Eamon

Rogena Mitchell-Jones, Literary Editor
RMJ Manuscript Service, www.rogenamitchell.com

Published by Mordant Media, Portland, Oregon

ISBN: 978-1-949316-46-9 (Print)
ISBN: 978-1-949316-47-6 (eBook)

10 9 8 7 6 5 4 3 2 1

CONTENTS

Powder

ACKNOWLEDGMENTS

Legitimate and thorough research, not just haphazardly scavenging tidbits from the internet, requires both time and a team of experts. This process cannot be rushed.

In certain cases, these can even be the heroes of society —librarians.

But sometimes, it's the people we encounter or reconnect with within our own lives that can be the key to unlocking our understanding. The inspiration to write this book started in a casual conversation with an old boss and friend I worked with over three decades ago.

A simple question led me to discover real-life reasons the FBI might investigate someone. Chris's answer was: "Remember those set dummies? What if one of them turned out not to be a dummy?" He was reaching back to an old *Twilight Zone* or *Outer Limits* episode where the wax statues in a wax museum turned out to be murdered people. And if you understand decomposition, you know the premise was shakier than the San Andreas Fault running through California. But I could work with the postulation.

That initial conversation turned into two amazing days of deep-dive education about the spacesuits of the Apollo program, including the half-hour of being helped into a suit by Global Effects very own Wes Brooks. My wing girl and consummate science nerd, Blake Stone, got the ACES suit treatment. We know how Howard Wolowitz of *The Big Bang Theory* felt. So we finished the last day with dinner at—you guessed it—The Cheesecake Factory. How could we not?

So, a tremendous shout out to Christopher Gilman and Wes Brooks at Global Effects Labs.

Two SAG-AFTRA actors, Danielle Rayne and Tommy Schultz, helped me navigate the intricacies of Hollywood. I wouldn't have navigated (the intricacies of Hollywood) without their patience and kind guidance.

For more of Danielle Rayne, she is the amazing voice of the Nash Running Bear series on Audible.

1
WTF

THE AIR HUNG heavy with stagnant heat. Even the shimmers rising from the New Mexico desert moved slower. The buzzards stopped circling over the animal carcass. Hopped on the ready-to-melt asphalt and flew away, searching for a cooler place to wait out the hot day. It was the kind of heat creating mirages or people seeing things that weren't real.

"Billy?" The girl whispered, scared someone would hear or, worse yet—shoot. "Billy? What are you doing? You're going to get us killed."

He glared at her through long, sweat-stringy hair. "Chillax, would you? There's nobody around, or we would have seen a car." He returned to continue picking the lock in the door with the paper clip.

The blonde rubbed under her T-shirt, drawn tight over her large breasts, so the words Lake Tahoe looked more like La hoe instead. She didn't understand why it was Billy's favorite, but if he liked it, she was happy to wear it—or take it off for him.

"I'm sweating." Her whine did not affect the young man fumbling with the door. At least the porch had a roof and the most shade the ghost town offered along the dirt street.

She stepped to the edge and leaned against the post. Looking from one end of the long porch to the other, she wondered what kind of building needed so much space. Her gaze stopped on the third window of the many windows.

"Billy?"

He mumbled the same distracted sound he used when he worked on his car. She didn't know if he was calling his car *Baby* or her. He bought her nice things like black lace panties, so if he called his car *Baby*, she guessed it would be okay. "Yeah, Baby?"

She turned and studied his sweat-stained T-shirt. She liked how his muscles rippled when he worked on his car or lifted weights. "If you want to get inside. How come you don't crawl through the window?"

"The windows are all locked, Baby? I need to pick the lock like I'm doing here." He swore under his breath. "Go see if we have any more water in the car, okay, Baby?"

"Okay, honey."

She rolled off the post and strode along the porch. She paused at the third window and peered back to the brunette kneeling at the door. Her closed-mouth smirk muffled a tiny snort. A prank would pay him back for all those he'd played on her.

Slipping through the opening of the window, she climbed inside. Careful to tiptoe, she snuck to the door. She could hear Billy swearing on the other side as she turned the knob.

The door continued to open wider until it revealed her shiny, wet-looking black leggings above the white tennis shoes. Billy raised his face and looked at the swollen Lake Tahoe.

Smiling down at him, the same as when she would bring him his coffee in the mornings, she spoke, "I climbed through the window. Funny, the lock thingy's missing in here."

Billy stood and snaked his head around the edge of the door. She was right. The guts of the deadbolt were missing. Only the handle worked. He only needed to turn the knob, not pick the lock. He looked at her smile and simpered one back.

Random heaps of tables and chairs piled filled the large room. It looked like the aftermath of a wild party. Desert dust covered everything.

"Whoa, Baby. Look at the old-timey bar. This must go back to the cowboy and Indian days. I wonder why it all got left here?"

They wandered around the stacks of furniture.

Her trembling hand hovered over the bar, hesitant to touch any surface. She couldn't shake off the images from all the horror movies she had watched as a younger kid. Even though they were in a building in the middle of the desert, it still felt like some remote cabin in the woods. Billy had stumbled upon the town after endlessly studying his Google Earth on their TV screen.

They borrowed his brother's Jeep for the long weekend and drove around to find the dirt road to the old ghost town. She only hoped they didn't have to sleep in the vehicle. The back seat didn't look comfortable.

She rolled her eyes—Billy had found the bar of his dreams. A full bar and no bartender to keep him away from the bottles. She strolled into the next room, where a large white thing was under a spotlight.

A body.

"Billy?" she whispered, unable to take her attention from the man sprawled over the crushed pile of chairs and table.

"Billy?" If the body moved, she would run and not stop until she reached Albuquerque. She sucked in a ragged breath. "Bu... bu... Billy!" The scream galvanized her resolve. The body wasn't moving. "Gosh darn it! Billy!"

"What?" He stopped by her side.

She pointed at the heap of broken chairs, table, ceiling, roof, and man.

"Him." The man's white suit glowed iridescently in the sunshine streaming from the hole busted through the roof.

Billy leaned in. The face behind the helmet's cracked face mask wasn't moving. The left eyeball had popped from its socket and lay staring at him. "Holy butt knuckle."

———

Deputy Zapata Yazzie of the Gallup Sheriff's Department had listened to the agitated caller. Scratchy cell service, so he wasn't certain he'd understood what the man had said. The sheriff sent Zap to investigate. He hated driving anywhere north of Yah-Ta-Hey. The territory was more Navajo than Zuni, and he couldn't remember which spirits to talk to and which to ignore. The closer to Ship Rock, the more his mother's voice shrieked in his head. Zap preferred sitting at the desk, watching reruns of Three's Company and the bouncing beach babes on Bay Watch.

He'd never been to the ghost town, but as a teenager, he'd heard plenty of horror stories. With his mother, Zap didn't need any white man ghosts in his head. It was full enough with his own.

Flicking the blinker, he slowed. To him, the road was as obvious as the entrance to a freeway. He'd avoided it most of his life. Zap drove the old Jeep Cherokee onto the sand, where the yucca tree leaned drunkenly against a cactus, watching.

Zap considered flipping off the yucca and cactus but was afraid he might piss off the prickly spirits. He gripped the steering wheel at ten and two and glowered at the sand ahead. If the old Jeep got stuck, he wasn't sure if help would come this week or next. He would miss Raymond Burr, the second part of a two-part case.

As he drove up the main street, he didn't feel so alone. By the tracks, he could tell the city Jeep used four-wheel drive. The white oval on the bumper contained the letters ABQ. *Tourists.* Further afield than Zap. Hopefully, the reported dead body was a prank.

A girl, her chest bouncing under a tight-fitting T-shirt, jumped up and down in the middle of the street and waved. Zap groaned as he turned the key and opened his door. He didn't need his dead mother screaming to know this would not end well.

"He's in here." She gestured toward the building to her left.

Zap waved from a block away. Certain the woman couldn't see him, he shook his head softly. His gut told him if there were a dead body, it wouldn't come back to life whether he walked or ran and sweated in the heat. And he damn sure wouldn't sweat for some woman from the city too stupid to use sun protection.

He passed several structures as he strode toward the woman. For years, he walked real ghost towns, ones that boomed and busted before the Civil War. Those ghosts weren't here. Just the nailed siding, planks, and batten told him the same builders had built this town.

The woman bounced back toward the building. "Come on."

Zap stopped six feet from her. "What seems to be the problem?"

Her hands moved in a constant flow, showing him where to go. "The spaceman's in here." Her hysterical voice gasped for breath.

Zap mulled over the one word everyone in the southwest used as a joke. "Is he green and about yay tall?" He held his hand at his hip.

The girl's arms froze in their wild gesticulation and fell limp to her side. "It's not a Martian, asshole. It's one of ours."

At the sight of the large boots, Zap stopped rolling his mental eyes. He recognized the astronaut suit from the Apollo moon landing. The straight-bar-patterned soles reminded him and every school kid in the eighties of watching music videos. The poster of the footprint is probably still hanging on a few bedroom walls or offices to this day. Zap had even seen the footprint tattooed on a guy's calf. He swallowed hard.

Pulling his phone out, he took photos. The dusty white suit glowed in the sunlight. He circled to the end of the pile of wood and lumber near the helmet. He took a photo of the layers. The two-by-fours could be part of the roofing or the ceiling. The crumbling plaster and thin boards of timber were the same ceiling material as the cracking lath and plaster in his own house. But there was no roofing. Whether it was cheap torch-down tar sheeting or tin—it was missing.

Glancing up, he confirmed the construction of the hole above him. He glanced around. Something in the room's airspace seemed wrong. There was no balcony or mezzanine floor to justify such a high ceiling or all the exposed beams. Shrugging, Zap pulled at the legs of his pants and kneeled.

Under the ceiling materials was the last layer. The table had broken along the center, where it had crushed over its middle pedestal. Broken chair parts looked like bits of lettuce, pickles, and carrot sticks in a crazy sandwich. Everything corroborated a heavy object crashing through a roof and ceiling, crushing the dining table and chairs. But no roofing...

Zap slowly stood. And then there was the heavy object. He looked through the gaping hole in the roof to the blue sky.

Where the hell did the man fall from?

2

STUFF

BURBANK 1957

Sunshine on San Fernando Road never bothered the ghostly elephant looking over the tall fence. The elephant was a landmark through torrential rains of the short Southern California winters and news crews frying eggs on sidewalks during the summer. The fiberglass ears flared slightly away from the body as the head and the upper part of the tusks floated above the fence. The four-foot-tall letters exclaiming taxidermy drew a smile on Valentine Diego's face, a smile every parent is familiar with on their child's face when they walk past a candy store.

Valentine pressed the door closed on his new Corvette. It was two years old but new to him. The original owner had needed cash as he ran from the hounding investigations by the rabid McCarthy crowd looking for communists. The man sold everything he owned and took his new bride to live in Mexico. Valentine gave him the thousand dollars he had earned the month before and wished him well. The car had four thousand miles on the odometer. It was a Hollywood car. It drove to the set in the dark and then exhaustedly back home in the dark or at daybreak.

The sheep bells clambered as the top of the door struck them. Valentine had bought a set of them for his back porch when he worked a small part in a western. The dunes were across the wide valley from Bakersfield but near a stock supply for the ranchers. Valentine's bells had already been changed to catch the breeze and softly ring. He was hoping to go back and buy more if his agent could get him more work on filming a new movie in the area. He had been learning how to drive a two-horse team chariot.

The young woman glanced up from dusting the many standing animals. "Afternoon, Val."

Valentine pointed his finger gun at the owner's daughter. "Look out, Betty. There's a leopard behind you, looking for some tender dinner."

She waved her hand down through the air as he walked into the back workroom. Sighing, she twirled the turkey feather duster around the wolf's head. "The only ones giving me the time of day are you guys." She looked at the three red foxes sitting on their mountboard. "And even you guys don't know how to Foxtrot."

Valentine lifted the apron from the bent deer hoof coat hook. "Afternoon, Will."

The man with a wild head of white hair and matching walrus mustache glanced up. "They must have wasted more film this morning." He flipped the tiger's skin away from the fiberglass leg. Brushing more glue the length of the leg, he gently pulled the skin back over the form and glue.

Valentine stopped at the work table, studying the pelt and size of the beast. "Solomon's?"

Willian sputtered some guttural swearing in Yiddish. "The pisher. The stupid fuck blew his money going to Bali, then got cheap. He paid for the curing, and then they stuck the crap on a slow boat home." He flicked his head over his shoulder. "The crap's on the table over there. It's a pile of shit. They over-cured the back half, and the tiger shrunk to the size of a house cat. The neck has salt rot from the slow shipping in a leaky container. But I had this skin from a zoo in Cincinnati who wanted to preserve their baby... until the mayor heard. So I got a gorgeous, cured tiger skin for free. It's a couple of hundred pounds larger than what the producer bagged on his canned hunt, but it will be impressive in his entrance hall. And impressive is all he'll notice."

Valentine nodded. "Ah, the secrets of us little people. Am I still working on the horse's skin?"

The man smirked at the shared understanding between those who work in the shadows and the bit-part actor. "Yes. Be a good brownie and scrape the fat off. I'll be over in a bit, and we can stretch it over the armature."

Valentine gave the man a two-finger salute and winked. "Aye, aye. Brownie fourteen horsing around as ordered."

The old man chuckled under his prodigious mustache. The silent movie scene played in his head. Valentine had only been five when he got the part to play a brownie who came at night to the old cobbler's shop and made the shoes. His screen credit was brownie number fourteen. Nobody remembered they had only hired six children and double-filmed them but paid them as one.

The cacophonous whirring of the chemical vat's fan echoed in the metal warehouse, making Valentine drowsy. He often fantasized about recording the sound to play back when he went to bed, but alas, he didn't own a recording machine. So, instead, he memorized the sound to use as a sleep aid at night.

With a grunt, Valentine slipped his stocking feet into the tall rubber boots. Donning his thick rubber apron and sturdy gloves, he prepared for another grueling day of physical labor. He pulled an end of the heavy hide from the bubbling liquid in the vat and meticulously draped it along the suspended bar. Anchoring it with clips to prevent any mishaps, Valentine made his way to the end of the vat and began cranking the massive iron wheel. Slowly but steadily, the bar ascended until the hide hung completely hoisted from the vat. With practiced precision, he waited for the dripping to cease before continuing with his task.

Valentine pulled on the large wheel and methodically moved the contraption away from the vat. Guiding the machine, he pushed the hide to hang over a sturdy mesh bed. Starting at one end of the bed, he carefully spread out the wet hide until it covered every inch of the bed. He then returned the crane to the tanning vat before returning to the washing bed. Removing his gloves, he tested the temperature of the water with his bare hands. Too hot, and the hide would shrink. Too cold, his hands would freeze, and he couldn't rinse all the acid from the hide. Taking up the long-handled brush, he began washing away the acid solution from the hide with deliberate movements.

As the hide rinsed to a light cream color, Valentine put the stiff-bristled brush aside. He lowered the second wire table on top of the first—sandwiching the hide between. Setting the two locks, he rotated the table so the hair side of the hide faced up—ready to be washed. Raising the wire mesh away from the hide, he took back up the brush and hose. He thought about his learning to ride as a young boy. To pay for the lessons and riding, he washed and brushed the stable's horses. He never cared that three hours of taking care of the animals paid for only one hour of riding. Every minute, he was in contact with the giant beasts he loved.

Tanning the large palomino horse's hide was a straightforward job with the crane and beds, but it just took time. Valentine preferred the smaller animals he could wash in a tub. But the work was something he had always found close to magical.

He flipped the hide and pulled the top mesh bed off. Pulling the keeper pin on the large hinge plate, Valentine rotated the bed and skin until it was almost standing straight up and down. Now he could reach all the hide, and the actual work would begin.

Stepping to the small cupboard, he chose his favorite scraper. The slightly curved edge of the blade let him work the last of the fat off the skin. If left on, the fat would spoil and, therefore, rot the skin. Which was not what the customer was paying for. He gripped both sides of the handle and started at the top of the table. With each pull of the blade, a thin layer of tanned fat rolled in front of the scraper. The hide behind was closer to a dingy white than the yellow-brown of before.

Will rested his hand on Valentine's back. He could feel the heat of the overworked muscles. They stood admiring the clean white skin. "Do you have a casting call tomorrow?"

The man blew out a breath through pursed lips as he looked at the fan above. The shaking started slowly and then turned into a jerk as he looked back down. "No. I have a voice-over on Monday. But tomorrow, I think I only have a riding lesson with a certain yellow horse." He nodded at the hide.

"Good. Lay the blankets on and wet it down." He drew his watch out of his pocket and held it up. "It's already eleven o'clock. We thought about bringing some dinner back for you, but I remembered you're on some crazy diet. How goes the chariot racing?"

Valentine grabbed the wool army blankets from the shelf. He threw out each in turn to cover the hide. Turning on the water, he hosed the blankets down until he could see they were sticking to the hide. He glanced back at his mentor. "It's kind of fun once you get the hang of guiding four crazed beasts in a circle. But the horses they use, I wouldn't want to take Betty for a ride at Griffith Park. I'm not sure they were ever riding horses. But when you harness them and back them to the rig, all they want is to run."

The older man chuckled roughly. "But isn't that what a race is? Run like hell and stay in front of everyone else?"

"Sure." Valentine flattened his lower lip as he bobbed his head. "But if you're shooting a movie, who wins is already determined. And it's not always the better driver or man."

Will pushed on Valentine's shoulder. "Just don't flip the crazy sulky and get trampled by the guys behind you. I'll need you if the young actor is crazy enough to bring back the whole elephant. He has a hunting license for it, but it's a hell of a lot of skin to ship back from Africa."

Valentine turned off the water, and they stood watching the

water run off the blankets. As the drizzle turned to drips, Will pulled the keeper pin and rotated the bed back flat. "He'll stay plenty damp for a few days. Why don't you sleep in tomorrow? We don't open until ten, and Betty will take care of anyone up front. Have a nice brunch, and we'll stretch the pony when you get in. Besides, I want to finish the tiger's body tomorrow before I work on the head."

Valentine's smile grew. "Maybe I'll splurge and take myself to dinner down at the pantry tonight. I heard the violinist was back from New York. I could use some pleasant music while I stand in line. And I don't have a script to memorize. So..." He held his arms out wide.

Will chuckled as he smoothed his index finger along his walrus mustache. "The world is your oyster, my boy. Now, show me this wild new car I heard pull up this afternoon."

3

SC2SFMFO

TRUE SUMMER DRIZZLE in San Francisco was cold, freezing, or bone-biting cold. Muna snuggled deeper into her tactical jacket—thankful for the springtime warm mist. Andy had wound her signature long braid into a tight bun for the competition. The shooting photos didn't look enough like her with the glasses and bun, so she wasn't concerned about her parents recognizing her. However, the one picture of her accepting the gold medal could be of concern if her parents saw it. Or someone in their mosque or circle of friends put the name with the photo.

The photo dropped on her breakfast table, with a pen for an autograph, had disturbed her appetite. Even if it was Erin and his wife, she struggled with asking them not to display it in a public space. The obscurity of the tiny breakfast café had won, but she knew more would come the closer to the Olympics they got.

Life and her shooting had been so much easier a year ago.

When her parents visited her to make up for missing her birthday, they focused on her desk and the wall of monitors. Mike and Oz were adorable as they shared how the two of them did the messy lab work, with Muna only lending them a hand with the mountains of paperwork. As they had talked, her mother had eyed the over-the-top workstation on Muna's desk and the small single monitor on the lab's desk. Muna had known her mother's bullshit detector was ringing louder than a freight train, but she would never let on. Muslim women were used to keeping each other's secrets.

Andy stood a foot further back from the rain-splashed edge of the loading dock. His giant skull mug gently floated in his large hand. He took a sip as he watched the black figure turn into the walled parking lot. He had warned her it would rain, but Muna had insisted she would welcome what came. She walked more pensively than usual, but she didn't walk like a drowned rat. His Uncle Andy's sense was tingling, but he'd let her come to him.

Andy smiled as she started up the ramp. "At least the wet is warm."

Muna turned at the top of the ramp and walked over. "That makes it easier to turn to steam."

He studied her face as she stopped. The tension wasn't combative, but it was adversarial. "Not an enjoyable breakfast?"

Her mouth tightened as her face turned out to the rain and the way she had come. Her sigh was soft. "Did you get the paper this morning?"

He blinked at the gentle steam swirling out of his mug as he paused. His voice echoed in the half-empty mug. "It's on my desk. Rain or shine, it lands on the dock at four-fifteen every morning."

Her one eye narrowed as her head swiveled back. "Did you want me to autograph the photo for you as well?"

He nonchalantly shrugged, his ironclad skull mug still firmly in place. "The pens are in the cup as always. Sign or don't sign. It's all the same to us. We're just proud of you." He paused, narrowing his eyes suspiciously. "But I have to wonder if this's what's really bothering you?"

Her armored jacket sagged a notch as her lower lip sucked into her mouth, and the roll lightened. Her sigh was deeper, and her tiny *no* was more fitting for the Hello Kitty pajamas than the heavy armor of the agent. She drew a sharp breath and blew it out one more time as she turned. Muna shook her head. "No. No, it's not. My battle is three thousand miles away."

The skull lowered as he rocked. "Your folks. I can only imagine." He watched her as she walked toward the distant elevator. He wondered if she would even take the armored jacket off at her desk. The phone ringing on his desk stopped him from wondering if she slept in armor. Many times, he had wondered if she was talking to someone professional after the beatings she had taken in Colorado.

Muna's hand paused at the zipper on the tactical jacket. As her eyes scanned over the wall of information, her sigh was slow and shallow. The fifteen pounds of jacket and armor were weight and insulation but also a feeling of security. It had cost her four hundred dollars to upgrade the armor and tailor the coat to her body. Her hand dropped to the mouse.

She looked at the shipping designation. The time estimate was an hour away, but she hated surprises. Even the surprise birthday party her mother threw for her sixteenth birthday hadn't sat well with her stomach. The cake had lasted five minutes before being flushed down the toilet.

She opened the small app she had started when she was at Quantico. The cup of alphabet soup filled the ocean she was currently swimming in. More days than not, it was extremely soupy. PDQ was not the same as ASAP. She found they both worked, but only if FUBAR wasn't attached to the results.

She copied the letters out and stood. Her mind cleared as she stared out the wall of windows. In the distance, beyond the low hills, there was a patch of blue. Probably a few miles out to sea. She closed her eyes as she took three measured breaths. Opening her eyes, she glanced down at the jacket and unzipped it. The unzipped jacket projected a casual look. But the weight was still safe as a security blanket.

She rolled her eyes as she turned toward the autopsy room. "Mike?"

The two men looked up from the large mound of meat on the stainless-steel table. String hung from Oz's hands as if he was playing some perverted game of Cat's Cradle. The red tinted his neck.

Muna paused at the doorway. From the men's reaction to her catching them with their hands in something they didn't find halal, her curiosity peaked. She stepped deliberately around the table, studying the enormous chunk of meat being tied up. "I didn't think they made prime ribs this large..."

Mike silently watched the meat. Oz silently watched Muna as she circled.

Her eyes narrowed with each step. "I don't even think a ham can grow this big." She circled behind Oz and then stepped to the table beside him. "What's it stuffed with?"

Mike gazed at Oz. His face was a hallmark card of *"I told you so."*

Oz froze. "Boneless turkey."

Muna snickered. "The whole bird?"

Oz ground his head right, then left, and back to the center. "No wings. They don't cook well in the ground."

Muna thought about the bird. "What did you stuff the meat bag with?"

Oz's shoulders fell a fraction of an inch. "Lobster tails."

Muna raised her face as she glared over her cheeks at the meat roll. "How many tails?"

Mike cleared his throat. "Nine. The other three didn't fit."

Muna smirked at the old joke her father made about stuffing a turkey. "Did you take out the giblet bag first?"

Oz and Mike looked openmouthed at each other in surprised horror. "Giblets come in bags?"

Muna groaned. *Uncle jokes.* "We've got something showing up in an hour."

Oz nodded at the large wad of meat as he tied another knot. "It's the roaster."

"Roaster?"

Mike giggled uncharacteristically. "Well, it started as a thirty-yard, roll-off dump container. But now it's an in-ground luau roasting pit."

Muna lifted and showed him the sticky note. "And it's marked SC2SFMFO?"

Oz groaned as he cut the string and stepped to the end of the table. His mouth moved as he sounded out each letter. "Sealed container. San Francisco Medical Field Office... It's not the roaster. Where's it coming from?"

It was Muna's turn to giggle. "Probably from Nash. Well, it's her territory. Kind of. It's coming from Gallup, New Mexico."

Oz glanced at Mike. "When is Kalani getting here?"

Glancing at the big clock, Mike fluttered one eye. "He's about an hour late, so any time now."

Oz twitched a smile. "San Francisco time or Hawaiian time?"

The box just inside the medical examiner's office beeped. Muna backed up and struck the large red button with the heel of her hand. "Yes, Andy."

"We have a roll-off dumpster full of dirt backing up to dock three. Does anyone know about this?"

Muna giggled and then sobered. "Do not disturb the bodies. We'll be right down."

"Okay. And I have a FedEx Freight truck backing up to dock one..."

Oz nodded. "He'll probably need the power pallet skid if it's any size at all."

Muna pushed the large button again. "Andy, Oz says you'll need to bring up the power skid from the basement. We don't know what it is, but if it came freight... it's more than just a head or hand. We're on our way down."

"Okay. The garbage guy is wearing a Hawaiian shirt, but it hurts my eyes. Can you come put him out of my misery?"

———

NASH COUGHED A LAUGH. "WHAT TIME DID YOU GUYS finally eat?"

Muna groaned and turned her phone around to show the continuing excavation in the dumpster. "They're digging it out now. They buried thermometers in the turkey and the lobster tails. The turkey just hit one-sixty-five about five minutes ago. They started the excavation when it was at one-sixty."

Nash crunched on the baby carrot. Lele had approved late munching if it was healthy. "And have the guys opened the sealed container yet?"

Nash could see Muna leaning against the door to Andy's office. The calendars she could see through the security window never changed. Gorgeous, gigantic horses—always.

"We did for a moment. It's from the Gallup sheriff's office. Not you. But it's your case. Nobody else would touch this much outer limits twilight zone shit."

Nash groaned as Powder snuggled into the bed between her and Mina. "Body parts?"

Muna's face lit up. "Nothing so mundane."

Mina rolled over and turned the phone in Nash's hand. Her growl was inner beltway feral. "Define what is mundane about a body cut nine ways?"

"Hi, Mina." Muna rolled her eyes. "And it was only five parts. So technically, it was cut only four ways. But I misspoke. I should have said nothing as earthly as the body parts on the monument."

Nash took the phone back as she pushed her head deeper into the stack of pillows. "I don't think I'm going to like the sound of this."

Muna pinched the bridge of her nose. "Let's see if I can paraphrase the report correctly." She rolled her eyes. "The spaceman appeared to have fallen through the roof and ceiling. The body came to rest on top of the roofing material, the ceiling construction, and a table with seven chairs."

Mina turned over. "Little black girl lies like a Persian rug in the front room of a pawnshop."

Muna heard and giggled as she held her hand up. "Swear."

Nash leaned her head over to one side. "What did it really say?"

"The spaceman appeared to have fallen through the roof and ceiling. The body came to rest on top of the roofing material, the ceiling construction, and a table with seven chairs."

Nash's eyes narrowed. "If the spaceman is green, that shit needs to get right back down to Area 51 where it fucking belongs."

Muna shook her head slowly as she peeked over her phone. "I'll be right there, Mike. Everything but the crustaceans. I'm just wrapping up with Nash." She looked back at the phone and shook her head again. "Apollo mission extravehicular suit. Straight off the surface. Covered in moondust and all."

Nash straightened and frowned. "That's fifty years ago... What shape is the body in?"

Muna bounced away from the wall. "Like it had been logging some beach time in Hawaii. Oh... except for the one eye rolled out of the socket. I gotta spend some quality time with the boys. It's Andy's surprise sixtieth birthday luau."

Mina rolled back. "Luau? As in pig in the ground type luau?"

Muna smiled. "Exacta Mundo. The company that did the cooking is called Book'em Dan Ono Kin Luaus. The guy is from San Francisco Police, but he grew up on the big island."

Nash started laughing. "The next question is whether he does Washington, D.C. Good night, Muna."

Nash thought about the time difference and scrolled through her numbers.

The man's laugh was just on the edge of having fun and mania. "Magic Rick, Agent. I was just shutting down to have a late dinner date with my husband. What exotic place can I send you and Super Dog to?"

"San Francisco for now. Gallup later."

"Hills are a snap. Horsing around is going to take some work. I'll figure out your best Gallup flight and car situation tomorrow."

"Just flight. For this trip, Muna had better pick me up. We have a dead spaceman or something."

"I'll do it after dinner and text it to your phone. Go pack."

"Thanks, Rick. Say hi to Norm and have a great dinner."

4

QUIET ON THE SET

1957

AS THE DIRECTOR shifted in his chair from talking to the writer, he glanced at the camera. Putting the eyepiece to his face, he nodded. The assistant director raised the small megaphone to his mouth. "Quiet on the set, please."

The director waved his finger at the cameraman. "Rolling."

From behind, the sound director confirmed he was getting sound. "Sound up."

A young crewman stepped over and held up the clapper board as he watched the director.

"Slate it."

The crewman opened the board. "Wild West Men. Act one, scene six, take four." He clapped the board back together with a snap.

The director waited for the young man to withdraw silently. "And... action."

Eleanore clutched at the cowboy as she sank to her knees. Her hands slid down his back until she hung from his belt and gun belt.

"Don't go out there, Henry. They're nothing but killers. There's nothing out there for a good-hearted man. Only death."

Henry pushes his hat back with his thumb as he turns slightly to provide a quartering shot of his squared jaw. "Eleanore, nobody else is going to save this town. So I'm it. I don't like it. You don't like it. But some days, a man has to do what a man has to do. It's his lot in life."

She stifles a sob as she looks up. "But those notches on Chance's belt aren't from picking blackberries. He's a born killer and pure evil through and through." She moves her grip on his belt to only her left hand. The right brings her kerchief and smelling salts to her nose as she turns, slumping into a sit. "If you go out there, I'll be a widow before the clock strikes noon. How will I live the rest of my life like that?"

The camera moved in for a close-up of her weeping face and held.

She sniffed with a heaving chest, her exposed upper cleavage surging.

The director, leaning in, raises his hand and holds it like an ax. "And, cut." He sits back. "Excellent Mary. You almost had me ready to cry for you."

The second assistant director stood with the script rolled open. "Alright, Johnny, let's do a walkthrough on the front porch scene." He turned. "Clarence? Do we have the guy for the fall? I want to practice the shooting and fall."

The balding man in a bow tie waved at him. "Yeah, yeah. We got extras from the lynching set to come over. They won't be shooting until the morning."

"Isn't that Balkey's film?" The director looked around.

"Yeah. But it's a bit-part actor so that Balkey won't kick. It's the Diego guy. He's got his SAG card, so he can even make noise when he takes the bullet and falls."

The director waves his hand as he looks over the script with the writer. "Yeah, whatever. Just make sure he's signed all the forms and waivers. I don't want another one of those messes we had at Angel's Hospital last winter."

"Got it, Danny. Forms and waiver."

Standing on the balcony, Valentine poked gently at his mustache with his ring finger. The sunshine wasn't as hot as it would be when the lighting guy turned on the large bank of Klieg lights. The arc of the carbon rods could vaporize a doughnut before Craft could set out a plateful. Long days gave actors strange suntans under their makeup. But the large walrus mustache was threatening to fall off. And probably at the worst time.

"I swear, Val, if you push my mustache off your face one more time, I'm going to throw you off this balcony myself. Now leave it alone."

Valentine's finger froze as he glanced over at the makeup artist. "Jeez, Fred. It just feels like there isn't enough glue or something. I don't want to have it fall off when I take the fall. If I don't have a mustache in the rushes, they'll make me do the fall again. You know how it is. The bean counters are already banging on Tracy's door about the overrun. That's why I'm bending both of my cards. Most of the time, they only want me to use my Extras card and save my SAG card for when I take a fall or something. They've already cut out the bar fight. Even though all us extras were willing to do the fight and only take the SAG pay for the actual screen time."

Fred pulled the mustache away from the man's lip and dabbed some more spirit gum in behind the prosthetic. His thin lips twisted under the pencil line of a mustache. "Tell me about it. Did you notice I'm up here with you? In a minute, I'm going to put on a cowboy hat and pick up another pistol. What they were going to spend on a full team of makeup is now down to my sister and me. She doesn't have any cards, and I'd make more with one of your E-cards. But if I bitch or moan, I won't work until after Christmas." He pushed on the large mustache. "I added more spirit, so it should hold. Just remember to twist early and land on your back. I saw them stick a second mattress out there, so there's at least that."

Valentine hung his head. "Thanks, Fred. Sorry about them cutting the budget. And I don't mean to whine, but it's getting tough lately. When I got home from Korea, I was hoping it would be a little more..." He shrugged.

The younger man, with the shock of stiff dark hair, tapped his fist against the actor's shoulder. "Don't worry about it. I saw the new Corvette. I was wondering who would snap that honey up. Is it true he sold everything?"

Valentine's eyes drooped shut as he slumped and nodded. "We stood at his kitchen counter as I counted out the money, and he signed the pink slip. There wasn't a stick of furniture in the place. I've seen empty soundstages with more in them than his house. He said they were getting on the train with three suitcases."

Fred glanced down at the cameramen running the new tracks for the dolly. "Hollywood will survive. But for the life of me, I don't know how."

The actor stepped back to the small patch of shade. "Just keep your head down and your mouth shut."

Fred pulled an imaginary zipper closed across his mouth.

"And... action!"

The cowboy crashed his way through the swinging saloon doors. As the doors banged against the walls, the man took the last steps to the edge of the wooden sidewalk. He paused and studied the deserted dirt street. His right hand eased back and found the handle of his six-shooter.

He stepped down on the single step from the sidewalk and porch. The horse neighed in agitation. The distinct sound of a lever-action rifle clicked from above him.

Spinning, he drew and fired at the hombre in the black hat and thick bandito mustache. The man choked as he grabbed his chest and fell through the railing—breaking it as he fell to the street below. A large woof of dust exploded around the body. Tipping his white hat back on his head, the cowboy spun his pistol on his finger and slipped the weapon back into the holster hanging low on his belt.

"And... cut."

The director blinked a few times as he thought about the performance. He stood from his chair. "Say... um..." He turned and whispered to his production assistant. She checked her roster and whispered back.

Turning, he walked to the edge of the shallow pit with the two mattresses buried in it, where a couple of hands were helping the guy get up. "Say... Valentino, can we do the fall again? But maybe you don't drop the rifle. Bring it down to the street instead. Can you do that?"

Valentine winced as he straightened. He banged his black hat on his clothes—dusting them off. "Sure, Mr. Goldman." He pointed at the broken railing. "But this time. Can the guys put up a breakaway rail or at least something easier to break?"

The director had gotten the yes he was looking for. He waved his hand in dismissal. "Sure, Valley, why not? Let's just skip the railing. We've spent too much time on this as it is." He looked up at the assistant director. "Let's reset and run it again."

The assistant director pointed up at the railing. "What about the railing?"

The director mopped the air with his hand. "Fuck a bunch of railing. Just run it. It isn't even five seconds of screen time. We might have to cut it, anyway. I need a banana and some juice. Where's the Craft, girl?"

The production assistant spun on her heel. "Craft? We need a cold juice and a banana here."

The man behind the table thirty feet away called out. "Which juice? Orange, apple, or pineapple?"

The director snatched the script from her hand. "I don't care. Juice." He turned back to his chair and sat fuming as he thumbed through the next shot.

"Places, everybody."

"Quiet on the set, please."

The director waved his finger absently at the cameraman. "Rolling."

From behind, the sound director confirmed softly he was getting sound. "Sound up."

A young crewman stepped over and held up the clapper board as he watched the director.

"Slate it."

The crewman opened the board. "Wild West Men. Act one, scene seven, take two." He clapped the board back together with a snap.

"And... action!"

The ruggedly handsome cowboy barrels through the beat-up saloon doors, slamming them against the walls with a crash. Striding purposefully to the edge of the wooden sidewalk, he steps down to the street. His hand rests on the hilt of his pistol as he surveys the empty dirt street. Suddenly, a metallic click echoes from above and behind him.

Without hesitation, the cowboy whirls around, drawing his gun, and fires at the dark figure in black with a thick bandito mustache. The man lets out a guttural cry as he clutches his chest and topples off the balcony, rifle still in hand. A billowing cloud of dust enveloped his body as it hit the ground. The cowboy nonchalantly tips his white hat back on his head and twirled his revolver on his finger before returning it to its holster.

. . .

"And... cut."

The groans from the street are muffled. "Please let that be good enough," the dead cowboy mutters under his breath.

5

UNBOXING DAY

Nash turned on her phone from airplane mode. The text was
waiting.

You're L8. I'm @ curb.

Nash stood and leaned over toward Powder. "Your sister is
cruising for a spanking."

James stood in the galley, bouncing on his toes. "I'm going back
to Rio for the next two months. Please try to stay out of trouble
while I'm gone."

Nash shouldered her rucksack. "Vacation or flips?"

James shrugged shyly as he rolled his eyes and looked away. "A
little of both. Mr. Italy is coming over to take a break. So I'll maxi-
mize my downtime, and we'll play tourists."

Nash smiled at the cabin door. "Do you ever fly to Barbados?"

He barked a laugh. "I have thirty years' seniority, but not
enough for the emerald island. But I could take some vacation
time…"

Nash waved. "We'll let you know when we go back down."

Powder stopped and ran back to James. Sitting, she raised one
paw. They shook, and she turned to catch up with Nash. The nicely
dressed older woman stopped and rubbed her thumb on James's

cheek—wiping away a single tear. "That's the best thank you I have ever seen in my thirty-eight years flying."

James cleared his throat and licked his lower lip. "Good night, Midge. Great, having you on my flight."

She called back from the jetway. "Always good to see you, James."

A clinging dampness hung in the evening air. Not like it was raining, but it wasn't a dry summer either. Nash looked to her right, away from the port authority enforcing the curb parking. The tiny drift of steam or air at the tailpipe was the only giveaway the SUV's engine was running.

"You're burning fuel."

Muna bumped her butt against the side as she stood away from the SUV. She slipped her phone into her pocket and pulled a chunk of jerky out of the other pocket. "How's my sister?" She bent for her kiss on the cheek. Standing, she rolled her eyes at Nash. "I just pulled up from the texting parking lot. I haven't been here for more than a minute."

The port officer walked up with his hands, grabbing at his buckle. "Is this the VIP you've been waiting all evening for?"

Muna opened the back door. "Yeah. Thanks for being so patient with me."

The man winked at Nash. "Next time she camps on my curb for an hour, I'm going to have to write her a ticket or get her phone number."

Nash feigned shock and interest with wide eyes. "Why? Do you have a grandson who keeps halal? Then maybe her father and I don't have to have her stoned?"

The man choked on his laugh and waved them away. As Muna walked around the back of the SUV, he smiled. "I won't tell you about my boy if you're still looking. He's only seven. And I think he likes bacon too much."

Muna laughed. "Thanks, Jamal. But you know me. If they don't have a chance at the NBA, I'm not interested."

The man waved. "Good night. And the best of luck at the Olympics."

Muna stopped at her open door. "I have one more shoot to qualify."

He called into the air. "I have faith in you. We all do, Muna."

Nash grunted softly as they turned out of the airport and surged up the on-ramp. "Look at you. Little Miss, I have fans everywhere I go."

Muna grumped as deep as her voice could go toward Oz or Uncle. "The proper term is contacts. Important people to know out here in the real world of the field. Sometimes, it's us little people who are worth knowing." She flicked the turn signal and surged the lumbering SUV into the middle lane. The truck behind her canceled his signal to go around her—locking her into the slow lane behind the Amazon Smile. "I think it was Helen Keller who said: it is not the giant leaps of our admired heroes but the muted struggling pushes of each small person who edges our society forward each day."

Nash stared at her mirror and watched the truck disappearing in the slow lane, now stuck behind the three Amazon trucks, each pulling two large trailers into the city. "Think or know?"

Muna glanced over with floating eyelids above her warm smile. "Does it matter?"

Nash eased down into her seat as she pulled Powder to her chest, ignoring the soft moan of being distracted from watching the lights and cars on the freeway. "Only in a court of law." She buried her nose in the fur as she closed her eyes in thought.

The late evening dusk transitioned into the enduring yellow glow of the San Francisco night. The heavy armored glass and insulation muted the sounds of the cars and trucks on the freeway. Only the soft sound of the barely audible classical music filled the air— more white noise than music for enjoyment.

"What's the status of the body?"

Muna flicked the turn signal and transitioned off the freeway onto the Juniper Sera highway toward the Golden Gate and the west end of the city. She peeked over. "The sixteen-year-old who tried to hold up the armored truck with a 3-D printed zip gun, or the body they found in the wall cavity in Carson City?"

Nash yawned and then feigned shock. "Good gosh. Zips to wall foliage. I leave you kids alone for a few short weeks. Is this what you get up to?" She hugged an almost sleeping Powder. "Shh… not you, Baby. You're always good." She glared at the now chuckling Muna, turning left toward their favorite late-night restaurant.

Muna snapped a quick peek over at the fur-covered woman. "If you're asking about the astronaut in the sealed container… The note on the sealed baggie said, *Do not open until Christmas or Nash arrives, whichever comes first.* So it's still on the loading dock. We don't know how to get it upstairs."

As they pulled to the curb, Nash cringed. "Baggie?"

Muna hit the button, and the SUV shuddered to silence. Pulling the handle, she opened the door and checked the mirror before releasing the five-way harness. "Don't ask me where you find a giant Ziplock baggie in the middle of the southwest desert, but they did. They stuck the spaceman in the bag, sucked the air out, and zipped it closed." She slid to the ground. "Oz and Mike are still trying to figure out where they got an ISO airfreight container without markings."

Nash and Muna followed the dog as she nosed the restaurant's front door open. "Eyesore?"

"No. ISO is the International Organization for Standardization."

Nash evilly smirked as she held the door for Muna to duck under her arm. "That would be IOS."

Muna distorted her face into a grimace and shook her head. "Nah, that would be Initiating Other Searches—a one-way ticket to the dark side of the internet." She chuckled evilly, revealing a fence of pearly teeth. "The original comes from some fancy Italian organization with a name longer than my wish list of office equipment. But they shortened it to International Standards, and now even the

Italians struggle to say it without spraining their tongues. It's all overseen by an offshoot of the World Trade Organization, so you know it's legit." She waved to the bustling chefs in the kitchen, flashing a smile as she did so. In the corner, Powder sat at their usual table in the back. The rocking movement of her head showed she was doing her happy dance with her front paws.

AS THEY WALKED UP THE FREIGHT RAMP LATER, NASH restarted the conversation. "So we have some stranger in a cartel-sized baggie wrapped in an internationally approved shipping container?" They rounded the corner of the dock to see the subject sitting in the back corner. "Holy…"

The slender security guard leaned against the door of the small office. "Hey Nash. Here for your birthday present?"

Nash slowed her approach to the hulking silver cube sloped on the lower half of the two ends. The slopes conformed to the inside walls of an airfreight compartment of an airplane. Nash blinked.

Peter bumped away from the door. "It's called an LD-29. They used to be a little longer to fit into the 747s, but those got phased out. Now, the twenty-nine are shaped to fit under the seats of the most common airplanes flown by airlines—737s and the matching Airbus. She's just seven feet deep, taller than Muna in her shooting shoes, and the door is ten feet wide. If they stick a bed in there, they get an extra two feet of length. The average service life is just over fifty million before patch and weld."

Muna leaned her head at the man. Her eyebrow raised in a question.

He raised both hands. "I was a ramp rat for Alaska. Produce and durables out and stinkers in. I was in Seattle."

Nash frowned. "I get the food part…"

"Stinkers? Yeah, Iced cod, sockeye, Chinook, halibut, and crab. If the deck was sloshing, the containers got stalled on the deck up north. The ice melted, and the meat was worse than the smell. Not a lot, but it happened, and you never enjoy sushi again. Yours came up from the oven, and I don't smell a thing. Whatever they shipped, it's desiccated."

Nash twitched her head sideways. "It's a body."

The man burped a laugh. "Desiccated. Trust me."

Nash looked at Muna. Her eyes moved to the man with his hands in his pockets. "I'll trust you in the morning. But right now...?"

He tipped his head. "I hear ya. I started this shift at the beginning of my last shift. Andy is out sick. I think he's having puppies."

Muna smirked. "He's down at his dad's place. They're having a colt. One the size of this box."

Peter jerked his thumb back over his shoulder at the office. "Yeah. We have the pictures. Sleep tight, you two. See you at four-thirty if they don't find me a relief."

Muna pushed the elevator button for the fourth floor. "You didn't even want to peek?"

Nash leaned to the side and scratched Powder's ears. "After sleep, shoot, shower, and something to eat. But not necessarily in that order." She frowned as the door opened. "I think. Which..."

"Oz might be in room six. So, five or three. See you in the morning." Muna opened the door to two.

Powder curled up on the bed and waited for Nash to finish in the bathroom. As she returned, Powder rolled over with the blanket in her mouth.

Nash laughed as she unzipped her pants and sat to take off her boots. "Goofy dog. You can keep the blanket. If you want, I'll open the window and let it get even cooler." The boots dropped, one by one, to the floor.

Turning the phone over, she texted three purple hearts and laid it face down. As she unbuttoned her shirt, she heard the return message vibration. It was one-thirty in Washington.

6

CRACKED

1958

THE DOCTOR TOOK a drag on his cigarette and then pushed the butt into the already full glass ashtray on his cluttered desk. He blew out the smoke to one side in deference to his longtime patient. "I'm not going to sugarcoat this, Val. Those broken ribs aren't what's going to kill you." He pointed at the X-ray slides on the light panels on the office wall. "See the white fogging in your lungs? That's cancer. You've been complaining about a persistent cough. Well..."

The actor closed his eyes. He wanted to open them and see cameras, people, and a director with his finger in the air about to call, cut, and print it. He knew in his heart it wasn't so. The cough had been waking him up. He sucked lozenges at work to keep it from impeding a shoot. He didn't smoke, like so many others, but he had wondered about the fumes from the tanning vats. The tanning acid ate his clothes where the heavy rubber apron or gloves didn't cover them.

He opened his eyes and studied the man who had been his doctor since he moved to Burbank after the war. To get his E-card and work as an extra, he needed an annual exam from a doctor approved by the film industry. Doctor Simmons snarked at the fool who paid his vigor to the mooks who made movies and then charged him to go watch in the theaters. With each fall, cold or physical, they had become friends. Their mutual love for movies, good or bad, horror or drama, drew them to flutter around a common flame.

"Can you cut it out?"

The doctor reached toward his shirt pocket and the pack of cigarettes and then thought better of it. He shook his head softly and waved his hand at the X-ray. "Maybe if you had broken a rib a year ago, we might have caught it. But now... we'd have to replace both lungs. And who knows where else it's spread." He rested his hands impotently in his lap. "Down at UCLA, they are working on some drugs... but from what I see, they make you wish like you were already dead, and for what? An extra week? Month? Two months?" He grimaced. "If it gave you an extra year or five, I'd say it might be worth it. But now, all I see is patients in agony, throwing up, and losing sleep. They can't keep any food down, and they waste away until their coffin is the only weight they put in the ground."

Valentine shifted in the seat. He studied the wood grain on the front of the desk and wondered about the stain. He sighed deeply. Looking back up at the friend and doctor, he grimaced for a heartbeat. "Do you break the bad news to all your patients this way?"

The older man leaned back in his chair. It squeaked quietly. "On Guadalcanal... did your commander tell you it would be a cakewalk? That the sweet and demure Japanese would welcome you with open arms?"

Val's voice was soft and sober. "We would have laughed him off the ship. No. And I see your point. So what do you suggest?"

The doctor rolled his head over to look at the X-ray. "Go home. Get your house in order. Say your last goodbyes. You don't have time for a grand tour of Europe or anything, but is there anything left you always had a hankering to do? Then, do it. But, for damn sure, stop jumping off buildings. Let them throw a dummy off or something."

"They don't look right."

The doctor rocked back to sitting up. "Excuse me?"

Valentine shrugged his face. "The dummies. They don't look right. The dummy is just a stuffed doll. The legs bend wrong, and the arms flail about in the air. They have three elbows, so they must reshoot the sequence. It's expensive and a waste of time."

The pragmatic doctor blustered his lips. "Well, that's just stupid. Make a dummy with a skeleton that works right. Make it look like a human. What do you do with those animals you stuff? Do the bears look like some little girl's teddy bear?"

Valentine's one eyebrow rose. "Do you have a real skeleton I can borrow for a few weeks?"

THE TRAFFIC FROM DOWNTOWN LOS ANGELES HAD BEEN brutal. The city had torn up three places along San Fernando Road for major sewer repair. When William had become frustrated at a long backup, he had changed to the smaller street winding its way around Griffith Park.

The smell of fresh epoxy catalyzing hit him just inside the door. He cringed and looked over at his daughter.

She stopped dusting and shrugged. "Don't look at me. Val came in with a cart full of resin and catalyst, dropped a wad of cash on the desk, and pushed the cart into the back. It's been stinking ever since. Oh. And he also said he didn't work for you anymore. But you now worked for him. You need to talk to him."

William nodded as he paused. "I didn't see the Corvette parked out front."

Betty rolled her eyes. "Maybe he got a divorce?"

"He isn't married."

Betty growled at the screech owl coming in for a landing on a limb. "The car, silly."

"Oh."

William started toward the back. "What in the world is he casting?"

———

VALENTINE LAID THE ALUMINUM ROD ON THE RESIN. It sank about halfway. Putting the other form on top of the lower, He weighted it down and then wrapped the long rubber strap around the two forms. With everything secured, he poured the rest of the resin into the mold from the top. He nodded his head at William, who turned on the shaker unit, and the form vibrated. Val watched the resin suck down from the edge of the form and added more. When the vibration showed in the small pool of resin, he stopped pouring, and William turned off the shaker.

"How many of these skeletons are you going to make?"

Valentine leaned back against the other table. "Several."

"But I don't see why you need to make a complete skeleton in a dolly just to throw it off a building."

"I looked at one of the broken dummies over at Burbank Studios. They took a length of aluminum conduit this long." He held his hands along the mold. "The tibia. They tied a knot in a half-inch rope and then another pipe and another knot."

William rocked his head. "The thigh bone."

Valentine pointed at him and winked. "A two-by-four stud with holes drilled in the ends were the hips. The ropes, holes, and a tied knot. Those were the bones for the legs."

The older man frowned. "No feet?"

Valentine closed his eyes as his head bounced from shoulder to shoulder. "I've seen old outtakes where the body falls from a bridge, and the foot comes off. Or the head is facing down, but the arms are straight up behind."

William pointed at the form. "And casting the skeleton…"

"I want to experiment with the joints. See how I can make a more lifelike stage dummy? The film is getting better and better, but the dummies they throw out of buildings and off cliffs… are the same ones Charlie Chaplin used."

William panned out his face as his eyebrows raised. "It just seems like a lot of time and money spent on something you're just going to throw out." He snuck a peek at the serious Valentine.

William cleared his throat. "Throw out…"

"I heard you the first time." Val bent over the form and poked at the pour hole. The resin had set. "Let's see what we have." He unwound the long rubber strap.

Prying the two forms apart, they looked at the clear cast tibia. William pushed his lower lip out as he bobbed his head. "Looks good."

"Clearly." Val chuckled.

The older man smiled at the timing of the actor examining the knee joint end. "Will it work?"

Valentine took it over to the other bone. The drill had a narrow bit in the chuck. Lifting the drill, he found his mark and drilled the resin with four holes. Picking up a thin gray wire, he threaded the wire through two of the holes and then lined the joint up with the other clear bone. The wire went through the other bone and back out and into the third and fourth holes in the new bone. Valentine tied a set of knots in the soft wire. "This is leaded wire. You can bend it a thousand times in the same spot, and it still won't break. It never work-hardens or turns brittle. The garden and topiary people use it to train shrubs and trees to grow a certain way. Florists use a similar wire. If a funeral home or cemetery gives them the wire back, they can use it over and over."

With a grin, he deftly attached the transparent kneecap to the joint, intertwining its wires with the others. He turned to William and demonstrated the range of motion, bending the leg in different directions. The patella, now firmly in place, functioned as a barrier, preventing any forward movement of the leg.

"That works."

Valentine held up his finger. Walking over to the shopping cart he had borrowed from the market down the street, he pulled out two pieces of pipe connected by rope. As he bent the combination back and forth in every direction, he explained. "This is what the studios use now." He held up his hand. "But…" he pulled out a small disk from the cart, which looked like he had cut it from a soup can. Wires fed through the four holes. Vall smiled as he placed the formed disk over the rope joint and twisted the wires to secure them.

William smiled at the mechanical knee joint. "Does it work?"

Valentine let the top pipe bone fall back against his hand. And then, he held the leg forward, and the pipe swung down but stopped when the metal plate formed the stiff knee. "I'd say it works."

The older man frowned as he pointed at the mechanical leg and then back at the cast parts. "So why not just make this? Why waste the time and money on the castings?"

"I can build a better dummy, without a doubt. But I need to show the movie executives why it works. For the ultimate test, I'll have a friend film the dummy falling from various places to show how it looks."

William placed his hand on Valentine's hand. He had seen the young man get excited before, but not about something so esoteric and absurd as a stage dummy. They looked at each other and sobered. "What's really going on, Val? And where's your Corvette?"

Valentine leaned against the large table and gently worked the mechanical joint. The tip of his tongue wet his lower lip. "Will you hear me out all the way?"

Concern crushed the older man's face. "Of course. Why wouldn't I…?"

Valentine winced. "Because I have a request. Call it my last request, but I'm serious about it. And I want you to hear me out and then promise me you will do what I want."

"Now you have me worried. What's going on?"

"I'm dying, William. Not in a year or two, and probably not more than a month or two. But sooner. My cough… well, the cancer is all over my lungs. There's nothing they can do, and what they can do… I wouldn't wish on an enemy." He held up the leg. "So this…? This is my legacy. I've jumped or fallen off forty-seven places. I've landed on mattresses and in water, and none of it was pleasant. And for what? Less than two seconds on the film or thirty feet of film on the cutting-room floor. This will last."

7

BOXING DAY

THE THREAT of drizzle had held off as they walked. The large breakfast encouraged them to walk the few blocks out of the way to wander through the meandering pathway of Golden Gate Park. Other people with dogs pulled on their leashes and scowled until Powder didn't even look at them as she pranced by. Nash and Muna would nod as they passed. The occasional small gasp was a guilty reward. They knew the civilians would wonder about the two FBI agents and the dog for the rest of their lives. The six-inch white letters on the back of the black tactical jackets left no doubt. But San Francisco, and especially Golden Gate Park, were no strangers to drug sweeps by law enforcement teams. However, few knew that the job was for someone other than the FBI.

"How do you think you'll do?"

Muna winced a small tick. "I've shot against nine of the contestants before. So only six are a wild card. The gal from Colorado logs about as much range time as I do. She works part-time for a local gun store who keeps feeding her ammo. And she's good. I think we're both worrying about the nineteen-year-old out of Ohio. She's put up some bad-ass scores occasionally, but she's not consistent. But all I need is to finish in the top four, and I'm off to Paris."

The three turned into the back gate of the compound. Andy, Oz, and Mike lined the edge of the loading dock. Their mugs rose as if on a stick. Only Oz took a deeper sip. "And there are the wandering daughters. You know it's supposed to rain this morning."

Nash gave them a horror-struck look. "What? And spoil my new hairdo?"

Muna shrugged with lazy eyes. "Andy would just have to reweave my hair."

Powder stopped and danced her front paws as she kept glancing at the enormous aluminum box—the elephant in the room.

Andy threw the last few drops of coffee into the parking lot. "Gentlemen, I think you just got the definitive: we don't give a shit, notice. How about we crack open the Christmas present?"

Mike rotated on his mechanical leg. "Don't have to." He smirked at Andy. "We already did. It's a windup toy, Buzz Aldrin."

Muna stuck her finger and arm in the air. "To infinity and mystery." She glared at Mike. "I saw the photos. Buzz was a pasty white guy. This one has more Hawaii about him. More surfing, sand, and sun. Besides, Buzz didn't have a glass eye."

Mike frowned. "What photos?"

Nash nudged his shoulder with hers as she passed. "See. It pays to read the memos the home office sends."

Oz laughed. "You have a home office?"

Muna giggled. "Yeah. One without a bilge pump running twenty-four seven."

Nash jerked her head around. "Are you doing another haul-out?"

The man groaned. "Nah. We'll find it and patch it from the outside. It's only a weeper."

"I thought the haul-out you did last year was supposed to fix all those leaks."

Oz shrugged his face. "If it's not in the water, how are you going to find the leaks?" He grabbed the twist locks and turned them. The door dropped open.

Nash stared at the giant heavy plastic bag with what looked like a life-sized replica of the MTV logo. But she didn't think even Muna would 3-D print the astronaut this size. The reddish-gray dust hanging in the creases and cracks lent a heightened definition to the figure. It gave it more of a surreal look as the soft morning light lit up the interior of the shipping container.

Muna growled next to her. "He makes me want to turn my monitor on its side. Nothing is right here. The astronaut isn't supposed to be lying on its back. And the big plastic bag makes it look like a Christmas tree ornament to hang in a store to sell. The aluminum box isn't the right shape, but it also makes an ornament for sale."

"Or one of your little statues. Only bigger."

Muna sharply snorted as she glanced at Mike. "A whole lot bigger."

Powder stood on the door ramp. She sniffed a few times and then stepped back, sitting beside Nash. Nash bumped a burp of laughter. "Yeah. I know what you mean. So how do you want to get him out? And where do we want him?"

Mike leaned forward. "Well, first, I want the air exchange to work when I open the bag, and I am in a hazmat suit. So let's get him out on a pallet. We can use the power pallet jack to move him around. And the freight elevator will take the length."

Andy looked at the bizarre contents of the container. He raised the clipboard in his hand. "Peter left this note last night. Said from the shipping weight, whatever was inside would only weigh three hundred and seventeen pounds." He pointed at the heavy-duty pallet suspending the body. "Leave the pallet in the container, and just move the body, and you're probably down to under the three hundred. Maybe even two fifty." Bouncing with his foot on the door, he shrugged. "This ramp would hold the power jack and the body. So, with two of us, we can drag the bag onto one of our pallets."

Nash looked at Mike. "Want to go warm up your laboratory, Dr.

Frankenstein? Andy and I can manage this work. We'll let Powder and Muna supervise."

Muna turned and started toward the elevator. "I'll go down and get the pallet jack."

Mike stood, rubbing his chin. Nash frowned at Oz and turned to Mike. "What's wrong?"

The man blinked and finally looked at her. "Nothing. Nothing is wrong. I just wondered how you get a person out of one of those suits. I mean, it's not like we're in zero gravity or anything. And I seem to remember watching stuff on the TV where it took a few people getting the astronaut dressed."

Nash chewed on her lip for a moment and then chuckled. "Ask Muna. Maybe she can find you an instruction video on YouTube or something. Or just call NASA. After all, it's their suit and probably their missing astronaut. Don't you think?"

His eye rounded. "That's the point. I don't know. Somehow, I feel like I'm trying to play Chips D&D games on Sesame Street with the Hawaii Five-Oh crew. Not the new one, but the old one."

Nash dipped her head. "Like the square peg in the star hole?"

Oz softly snorted as he stared at the astronaut. "More like kicking the golf ball for a home run to win the rubber of bridge."

Mike held out his finger—pointing. "Yeah... and now I know I won't sleep tonight."

THE FOUR-PERSON LIFT HAD MADE SIMPLE WORK OUT OF getting the giant baggie and its contents up and onto the autopsy table. As Nash and Muna helped Mike into the hazmat suit with its self-contained air source, Oz turned on the large air evacuation system.

Oz hovered over the temperature readout. His eyes were fixated on the control and monitor of the four-foot-long catalytic converter lurking in the ceiling space above. The contraption could incinerate all pathogens or biologicals encountering its platinum and palladium web. But its reach extended far beyond mere toxins. Even the most volatile solvents would ignite and raise its burn temperature to a scorching three thousand degrees. Oz knew this chamber held immense power, and he couldn't help but feel a sense of unease as the fiery dragon hummed to life.

He turned and examined Mike. For this exercise, the man had opted for the total self-contained suit—usually reserved for fieldwork. "How's your oxygen?"

Muna stuck her thumb in the air. "He set the saturation mix to low. He's got at least an hour if he needs it."

Oz looked back at the gauge. "We're ready here. The air exchange is every three minutes. The web is standing at a steady cremate on contact. We'll monitor and watch everything from outside the door. How are you going to get in the bag?"

The suit's external speaker was tinny. "If the zipper doesn't work, I'll use the knife." He bent forward and felt at his stomach.

Nash grimaced. "What's wrong, Mike?"

The orange suit swelled and became puffy. He straightened, and through the face shield, his eyes were bulging. He turned and looked at Muna. "Does this extra-large suit make my butt look fat?"

Her eyes narrowed to slits as she looked at Oz. "You kill him. I don't want to get my hands dirty."

Nash turned Muna by the arm toward the outer laboratory. "We need lunch in Tiburon. Where does Mike keep his credit card?"

"Should we lock the other chucklehead in here with him?"

Nash barked a laugh. "Good idea. Then we can say it was operator error and a lab problem."

Oz glared at Mike as he shuffled past the now deflating orange suit. "You're on your own with that one." He closed the rarely used door and watched the seals change from red to green. "We're all green here."

Muna snorted as she sat at the computer with its dinner-plate-sized monitor. "Pumping in the sarin and laughing gases now. Please count backward from one hundred."

Mike's voice wasn't as metallic coming from the monitor's speakers. "I'm right here, you know."

Nash poked Muna's shoulder. "It's still twitching. Give it more of the ricin gas."

Mike ignored the teasing. "They fused the zipper shut. I'm switching to an oh-five scalpel."

Muna watched the monitors of the air passing through the catalytic converter. "You only have a decrease of oxygen. But there was an uptick in body gases. Did you fart? Or is the back of the suit always that ballooned?"

They watched the camera monitor as the suited figure continued to cut away the giant baggie. The figure shuffled to the other end of the table—cutting as he moved. "I'm at the bottom of the bag. Muna will be let down. There are no more pork rinds."

Mike continued to clear away the rest of the large bag. Bracing his one hand against the astronaut, he pulled the plastic out from underneath the body. Leaning forward, he appeared to be examining the boot. "Hmm." He moved to the end of the table and the other foot. "Interesting."

Muna heard or felt Nash's intake of breath to speak. She held up her hand as she shook her head and scowled. Her voice was almost silent. "Don't." Her eyes closed as her chin fell to her chest.

Oz cleared his throat. "What did you find, Mike?"

The figure on the monitor pointed. "These oversized boots."

"What about them?"

The suited figure straightened and faced where he knew the camera was. "Age-old question about the size of the boots and why they needed to be so massive."

Oz maintained his deadpan face. "Why?"

"Because of their gigantic feats."

Muna typed on the keyboard and then hit the enter key. The mechanical computer voice covered anything else being said. "I'm sorry. You have reached a non-working number. Please hang up and don't call back."

The figure continued his walking exam of the astronaut's suit. Lifting the hand and arm, he moved it around. "No evidence of rigor mortis." He moved back to the left leg. Lifting it, he bent it at the knee. The leg bent easily enough. "All extremities appear to be fluid, with no rigor mortis."

As he reached the head, he bent forward to a closer examination. Muna wiggled the mouse as she watched the frozen image. "Hey guys?"

Muna's one eye narrowed to a slit. "What?"

"Do we know how to open this suit?"

Her forehead smoothed as Muna turned to look at Oz.

His eyes turned wild as he shrugged with both hands rising in the air.

Muna rolled her eyes. "We'll get back to you."

Muna stood and walked into the other room to her computer. Connecting the one monitor to the lab's computer, she started her search.

Mike continued his examination of the entire suit and even looked at the face shield. Finally, he looked up at the camera. "Well?"

Muna's voice sounded like a high schooler explaining how their dog ate the homework. "I only could find a grainy two-minute clip of a guy climbing into an Apollo suit. But there were no instructions."

The suited figure moved to the cabinets on one wall. Pulling out a drawer, he held up a black box with three tubes coming out of one end. A green light lit up on the top. "Muna, are you getting the connection?"

She pulled a small panel up to the upper screen. It filled the large monitor. "I'm reading the background air, Mike. What are you thinking?"

"I'm thinking NASA won't like me very much." He picked up

the scalpel and made a minor cut on the chest area of the astronaut. He held the three tubes of the sniffer into the incision. "Anything?"

Oz and Nash could hear the curl of Muna's mouth. "Eww. Nasty. There is some serious locker room stench. We're talking about jockstraps and socks that are long overdue for washing, which is some kind of stench, but no decomp."

8

LEND ME A HAND

1958

THE THREE-STORY TALL WALL, running along Barham Boulevard in Toluca Lake, was the public wall of the Warner Brother's Studio. Some saw it as snobbery, others as a snub to those not in the industry, and those on the inside knew its major function was as a sound barrier to the modern world. The background noise of an emotional farewell scene between a young woman and her Confederate soldier wasn't the sound of a passing truck.

The studio painted the movie playbills gigantic to be eye-catching at the new speed limit of thirty miles per hour. Two posters featured James Stewart for Vertigo and Sophia Lorin in Martin Ritt's mystery film *The Black Orchid*. Nobody driving by needed to read a name. Only the movie titles stood lettered out on the walls.

On the other side of the thick wall, the office trimmed in dark walnut paneling and heavy furniture, was the stage for four men and two extra arms. The arms sat upright on the central table. One was little more than an enlarged hand of a Raggedy Anne doll. Three lines sewn in black defined the fingers on the stuffed mitten.

The thumb was flatter than it was wide. Someone could have cut its cloth from a flour sack.

The other hand was more human. Its arm, encased in a white dress shirt with a cuff link, protruded a precisely prescribed amount from the fine wool sleeve of the tuxedo. Latex fingers curled to hold a martini glass with a cast resin martini and two olives.

The movie was grainy but got the point across. The body fell from the bridge as the camera panned down. Dust exploded where the body landed. In the next scene, the body falls in slow motion from a fourth-floor window. The camera doesn't move but, from the distance, catches everything but the throw. The point of the scene is the sudden ending as the body hits and crushes the roof of a car.

Valentine points at the screen. "We had to load an extra two hundred pounds in the body and legs to make it crush the car."

The man in the three-piece suit turned. He removed the cigar from his mouth. "But that's not you."

"No." Valentine wagged his head. "The highest I've ever done without an airbag was two stories. The reason you don't see us throw the dummy is because we threw him from the seventh floor. So we're out of the camera."

The cameraman turned off the projector and retreated. His job was done. He knew Valentine would slip him a twenty later over dinner at the steak house across the street. Any mention of what camera had filmed the falls and where the film had come from was between the two longtime friends.

The three men turned to the arm standing out of the small platform. Valentine carefully took the martini glass from its grip. Grabbing the dummy's right hand with his, he gently curled the fingers to form around his hand. Holding the fake hand out to the head of the studio, he smiled, "Greetings. I'd like you to meet Dropper the First."

The man switched the large cigar to his left hand and shook. His left eyebrow rose as he evaluated the grip. "I've shaken hands with more breathing dead fish at the Oscars. How did you get it to feel so real?" He passed it to the production head. The man's reaction was the same.

Valentine took back the hand and arm. Gently curling the fingers, he rolled the hand into a fist. "I believe even this fist might stop a fight down at the Dodge City Saloon, with or without Mister Wayne and the boys. Just as each finger has the same bones as your hand, you can bend the connecting wires running through the plastic tubes more than a thousand times. None of the five wires in each finger will break." He reached into his pants pocket and pulled out a small hank of the same gray wires. "Here. This is the same wire. You can play with it or give it to your kids. If you can bend it so many times it snaps, I'll give you twenty bucks."

The man stuck his cigar in the side of his mouth and held the wire near the lamp on his desk. Bending it several times, he turned. "What kind of wire?"

"It's an alloy of lead and base metals. None of them work hardened. In fact, if you try to temper the wire, it just melts."

The gaunt production head leaned over to look. Giving him the wire, the studio head bent two fingers of the hand back up into the sign of victory that Winston Churchill had made famous. "So, how many dummies are you planning to make, and how much are you sticking me up for them?"

Valentine didn't hide his smirk. He knew how the industry worked and the sizable amount of money they spent on what they wanted. "A lot, but I'm only making seven dummies between now and next month. The eighth one, you won't get until after Christmas. During hiatus."

"But I'm getting them all?"

"Yes. And once word gets around, you'll be in the business of renting out set dummies. Ones who can take a fall off the new skyscraper on Wilshire Boulevard and just bounce into the next scene without going to the hospital."

"What's stopping us from duplicating them?"

Valentine reached out and rested his hand on the man's shoulder. "Reggie, you, and I go way back. In my first film, I was just a face in a crowd. But you? You were a freshly made assistant producer back then. Most people think you just appeared in the office, but I know you worked your tail off to be here. It's why I brought these to you instead of going over to Fox. You were one of us. In your heart, you still are." He paused and looked at the production head. "Danny, could you please give us a minute?"

The man looked up and glanced at his boss. The man nodded. Placing the wire on the table, he quietly slipped out of the room.

Valentine waved his hand at one of the lounge chairs. "Have a seat, Reggie, and I'll tell you why the dummies are going to cost you more than your new Cadillac and a mistress to drive it for you."

The man froze halfway into the seat. His face was halfway to horror. "All of them, or each."

"Each."

The man sat and made himself comfortable. Valentine stepped to the grand desk to fetch the gold lighter in the shape of King Kong's skull.

As the man puffed, relighting his cigar, he looked up at Valentine. "You are becoming more expensive than my wife."

Valentine snapped the flame shut and returned the lighter to the desk. He turned to take his seat. "Yes, but for me, it's only temporary."

9

CAN I CALL A FRIEND

THE SKY PULSATED A DEEP BLUE. Not an overwhelming, world-altering blue, but one you would expect on an ordinary summer day in any other city. You might even plan to spend your lunch break lounging in the park. But in San Francisco, this hue was different—it was the blue to tempt people from all over to visit and bask in the excellent weather. And yet, they would still complain about how unseasonably cold it was because they hadn't read Mark Twain's complaint about freezing during his summer visit to San Francisco.

Erin stood glowering out the window as Nash, Muna, and Powder slipped through the door into the café. Nash looked back out the window where the man was looking. "Tourists, little green aliens, or something more pleasant." Nash and Muna were beginning to understand the city natives' aversion toward tourists.

He turned. "I don't trust nice skies. The announcers at Candlestick Park in eighty-nine even commented on the gorgeous fall day. Then was when everyone in the stadium should have run. As the night turned out, we didn't get home until three o'clock the next morning."

Muna frowned and then nodded. "Loma Prieta earthquake. Yeah. Wiggly Field."

He glared at her.

She held up her hands. "Or so I've read. I wasn't born yet." She shied her head and batted her eyelashes. "Coffee…? Please?"

He turned. "We saw you three coming up the hill. Wife's already cooking."

Nash slid into the booth behind Powder. "Thanks, Erin." She looked at Muna. "Anything yet from NASA?"

"Honestly? I don't think they wake up this early."

Nash ruffled Powder's head and ears. "How about the higher authority?"

"Ming and Sweet Thing both pinged me back. They only found the same video clips I had found of the guy climbing into his space suit, but no close-ups. Even the earlier stuff, when they fully suited up for take-offs, didn't show any detail."

Nash leaned in over her coffee. Smelling the steam, she eyed the smaller agent. "Well, after all, it was hard to film everything in those days. They had to carve everything into the film with stone hammers and obsidian chisels." She sipped and leaned back with her eyes closed. "But in all fairness, it was all finished by the time I was born. And for your generation, it must have seemed like ancient history."

"The last flight was over fifty years ago. It wasn't like everyone had a camera in their pocket. Heck, even the smartphone isn't legal to drink yet. But three-quarters of the world has one. Steven Jobs thought they were going to put a computer in everyone's house. He had no idea it would be in their pocket instead."

Nash looked out the window at the blue sky as she fingered the fuzzy ear. "He should have listened to the wife who suggested adding sound to the first Mac. She's the one who saw the future."

"Yeah, but she didn't have the extra bits hanging between her legs." She glanced up at the man with the arm full of plates.

Erin chuckled. "I hear nothing, see nothing, and only have my wife's opinion."

Nash jerked her thumb over her shoulder at the window. "I would have thought the boys would be up and relishing the sunshine."

"They popped the roof open about the time we were getting ready to open. I think the platform rose with the sunrise. They must be planning a busy day. But they waved. I was totally jealous to see the table decked out with a rainbow tablecloth and fine china. Their rooftop dining gives me something to aspire to."

Nash adjusted her plate. "If you open a rooftop café here in the Sunset district, my wife might have to telecommute. We'd move here just for that."

The man rested his hands on his hips as he surveyed the table for anything missing. "Well, you have pros and cons to living anywhere. If you have enough money, you can build a dining room elevator up through your roof, so you get the view and eat alfresco, or you can come to eat at our restaurant."

"I like it when someone else cooks. Less cold cereal and charcoal."

"Enjoy."

Powder leaned forward to nibble at the first bite of her cut-up omelet.

Later, as they paid, Muna fished her phone out of her pocket. "Go for Agent al-Faragi."

She listened to the person on the other end. "That would be perfect. I'm in a meeting right now, so they can take their time, and I'll call you back on this number in about an hour. Thank you for finding the tech and having them come out of retirement to help us."

She shoved the phone in her pocket at the door. "NASA. They found a tech still alive who can talk to us."

"Where are they at?"

"Texas. Johnson Space Center. But the guy is a docent at the

Cradle of Aviation Museum in Garden City out on Long Island. His grandkids live nearby."

Nash glanced at her watch. "And he'll just fly over in the next…"

"Ass. Video. But he needs to be where we can link in or something."

"Why not just FaceTime them?"

Muna rolled her eyes as she turned the corner. "Some people are old. Flip phone old."

Nash barked a sharp laugh. "We FaceTime with Uncle all the time. It's Bradey who has the flip phone. And I think I caught you looking at those new flip or folder phones."

"I'll wait for a couple of generations. The fold is the weak link."

"What was Mike's final analysis last night when you two knocked off?"

Muna shrugged as they started up the last hill. "He'd just as soon do it the standard medical examiner way." She held up her hand and two fingers snipping.

Nash grumped as they turned into the gate to the FBI compound. "It would save time."

"NASA wouldn't like it if this turns out to be one of their precious missing EV suits."

"How do you lose a suit like the big guy? Just lay it down somewhere and forget where it is?"

Muna glanced over as they walked up the ramp to the loading dock. "Everyone sat on the edge of their seats and watched a grainy video of Neil Armstrong stepping off the ladder to the surface of the moon. We all know what he said about the step for mankind. But nobody was thinking about preserving that historical piece of video."

Nash frowned. "I've seen it. At least a dozen times."

"Yeah. Now. But NASA didn't save it. The major networks didn't save it. They all thought someone else had saved it. But nobody did."

Andy stepped out of his office with his giant skull mug in his hand. "You guys talking about the lunar landing tape? One small step…? The one they found in Antarctica?"

Nash squinted. "Antarctica?"

Muna snorted softly. "Yup. They had sent a movie copy down with a bunch of other stuff. They would have shown the film a few months later, but at least the crew down there got to see it. Then, they stuck it on a shelf. It was one of those things nobody thought about, but they always celebrated Lunar Landing Day. Go figure."

Andy pushed his mug forward and finished, "When everyone was freaking out about the video being lost, the crew in Antarctica asked if anyone wanted a copy. The original is still down there. And they still celebrate the other intrepid explorers."

Mike and Nash had rigged one of Muna's monitors on the other autopsy table. The monitor didn't have a camera, so Muna jerry-rigged a drone camera to feed the observation. They had slaved all the hanging autopsy microphones to go hot to whoever was nearest and talking. To assess, they had called Ming but got Bunny in an empty command center of Deep Six. "The kids are having a picnic on the beach. Baby and Petey turn eighteen and sixteen this month, so they opted for a picnic. I hate sand… So…" She held up her hands as she slowly turned around in the cavernous room full of blank computer screens. "Here I am." She leaned in toward her computer. "Is that a dead astronaut? It looks like Neil Armstrong. Or another guy."

Nash smiled at the woman who got the same history lessons she had. "Right period, same suit, but wrong guy. We don't know who this one is, but we need help to get the suit off him without destroying it worse than Mike already did. We were just checking out our rig to make sure everything works. But we have NASA calling any minute now. But good to talk to you." She waved at the fading image as Muna switched to the incoming call.

Muna took the call on her phone. "Go for Agent al-Faragi."

"Hi, this is Dick Sharp from NASA. Texas said I was to call this number for a Zoom call?"

"Hang on, Mr. Sharp, I'm transferring you into the autopsy room."

The man was sitting at a desk with spaceships, photos, and models behind him on shelves or hanging.

Mike smiled. He recognized a man whose identity intertwined with his career. "Good morning, sir. I'm Mike, the medical examiner who can't figure out how to open your handiwork."

The man chuckled. "Our connection device is incredibly simple and brilliant. The helmet, gloves, and boots are all connected to the suit in the same way. A dogged ring twisting to lock. So let's start with the helmet because it's exposed."

Mike sidestepped toward the ring around the neck, gesturing toward its intricate lines and markers. "I was trying to get the little arrow to switch from zero to three bars, but the ring wouldn't budge."

The man pursed his lips and tipped his head to one side. "Ooh… so close, and yet so far. First, see the block just below his chin? Yeah, the square one. Pull, and you'll feel a click as it unlocks. Now turn the ring to the three bars, symbolizing separation. But to the third bar."

Mike leaned in and turned the ring. "Okay?"

"Did you feel the ring expand? Those were the dogs moving out from the ring on the helmet. Now place your thumbs on both sides of the ring and push away from each other. But be careful not to choke the astronaut. Remember, Uncle Sam has almost a billion taxpayer dollars invested in each person they shoot into space."

Mike applied pressure, and the ring separated. "Got it."

"Great. Now, if you remove your thumbs, you will see the ring close back together."

Mike pulled his hands back and watched the ring snap back together. "Clever."

"More than merely cleaver. Magnetism creates the perfect seal. But it doesn't provide security. So, they have the dogs in the rings. If all six of the dogs don't seat, you can't lock the ring."

Mike held up the gloved hand.

"Pull the gaiter down onto the glove. The gaiter was there on the gloves and boots to protect the rings and create a smooth transition to the arm and legs."

Mike pulled down the extra piece of cloth and elastic band. He smiled at the familiar ring. Turning the ring, he separated the glove from the arm and carefully drew the hand from the glove. "Slick as a banana slug in a spring rain."

The man in New York chuckled. "I'll take your word for it. We were visiting one of the California universities several years ago. The bookstore was selling cans labeled Cream of Banana Slug. I figured it was better on their shelves than mine. But it was memorable. Now, once you have the helmet, gloves, and boots off... you'll need to sit him up and detach the life support on his back. That will expose the large zipper system to get the astronaut out of the suit."

Mike straightened. "Thank you for your expertise, sir. If you ever are out this way, stop in, and we'll give you the nickel tour before taking you out to lunch."

"I don't travel much anymore. And I don't do well with anything to do with blood. But I appreciate the offer. You have famous seafood, almost as good as the lobsters we get from just up the coast. But feel free to call if you have any other questions. Oh... also, marked on the rings is the suit ID number, so we knew we had all the right parts matching. Lunch awaits." Mike reached out and pushed a button, but the screen turned black.

10

WHO IS THIS?

THE GLOVES and boots sat on the enormous expanse of the six desks pushed together in the office room. The afternoon sun, streaming from the still blue sky, gave them the neon glow that had been the hallmark of so many newsreels in the nineteen sixties and seventies.

Nash looked around for the helmet. She knew she had brought it out and put it down next to the small 3D-printed rocket ship. It wasn't an Atlas rocket, but Flash Gordon's ship would have to do until Muna found an STL file to print an Atlas. "Hey, Muna?"

The response was muffled. Almost as if Muna was face down in a trash can. "What do you need? I'm kind of busy here."

Nash walked around the wall of six large monitors arched over two Truman-era desks. The helmet almost swallowed the young woman's head and shoulders. She had to push it back on her shoulders to look out of the visor. She pulled the dark, gold shield forward to show. The helmet turned to face Nash.

Nash turned to see the monitors broken into the dozen zoomed faces of the girl squad of Deep Six. "Oh, yes. I see how busy you are showing off evidence critical to an ongoing investigation."

Ming raised her hand. "Of which we're already sworn in as research investigators."

Sweet Thing waved her hands in a time-out move. "Excuse me. But I found the video of the guy getting into the suit."

Nash lowered her head. "And which one of you found the instruction manual for opening the suit to get the body out?" The Zoom blocks went dark one by one until there were just Ming and Tree.

"Lucky break finding the guy who knew about the rings."

Tree nodded. "It's amazing how many billions of dollars got spent in the space race, and yet, so much of all the research and expertise just got lost or thrown away. We got to the moon. Okay... moving on to the next set of toys."

Muna opened the face shield. "Yeah, the space station and research. They could monetize the research. But the moon sucked billions to send some stick jocks to play golf on the big golf ball in the sky—no research. What they learned about getting there, they forgot. And now the hardest thing for them to do is to sell going back. Or worse, going to Mars."

Ming rolled her head. "I'd rather go dig up a river."

Tree pulled her long blond ponytail around and stroked it down her chest. "So, what have the boys learned about the body?"

Muna and Nash shrugged in unison. "We got locked out. Muna helped get the gloves and boots off, and Mike handed me the helmet. We brought them out here, then went back and found the door to the autopsy locked from the inside. That was yesterday. Today, they went in at nine and haven't even come out for a lunch break. Whatever they're doing or finding, they're keeping to themselves. We thought about just leaving a note. Gone to the beach. Call us when you want to share."

Ming smiled. "Is the beach on the roof of a four-story building in Orange County?"

Nash leaned her head forward. "With this kind of treatment, it might be a beach of pink sand in Barbados."

Ming looked at Tree. The blonde growled. "Don't get any ideas. They only have two ports, and both are already being dredged."

Nash sighed. "Well, I'm hungry, and I don't feel like wasting this blue sky."

Muna pushed the helmet up and held it above her head. "Sounds like the deck in Tiburon, ladies. We'll talk later."

Nash took the evidence and polished the gold sun shield with her sleeve. "Later, girls. We'll let you know where the beach is when we find out."

Muna looked at the dark screen and frowned. Standing, she stepped to the side of her wall of electronic information. "Find out or decide?"

Nash placed the helmet in the sunshine next to the boots. "Find out or decide what?" She turned to face Muna.

"You said when we find out. As in, we're told. Not where we decide to go."

"Go where?"

They turned to look at Oz.

Nash sat on the desk with the sunshine behind her. "The beach. If you two keep playing secrets from the team, we're taking our marbles and going to the beach."

The man hummed. "Sand, maybe. But I don't think there's a beach there." He turned and scooped his hand through the air.

The body lay covered on the examination table. On the end wall, the X-rays of its hands and feet glowed as strange constructions. Nash paused at the films. The shadow outline looked positively like a hand, but the bones not so much. The foot was even more not what she expected. Mike stood by the computer screen Muna referred to as the Mini-Me. But at twenty-seven inches, it was large enough to see what Mike and Oz had worked on.

"Is this a crash dummy or something?"

Mike yawned as he held up his finger. "We apologize for the secrecy and locking you two out. But we wanted to go through this step-by-step to see what we had before opening it up to you two."

Muna leaned closer to the screen. "Are the finger bones wire?"

Oz cleared his throat. "Okay, let's start with the hands. The answer is yes—you're looking at wires. But if it were only the wires, the fingers would flex in a curve or ball. So, small aluminum tubes create the bones between the joints." He reached under the white cloth and pulled out the left hand. Bending the index finger, he pointed out the straight sections of the finger between the knuckle and the first finger joint. He pointed along the back of the hand and then at the X-ray. "You can observe the faithful duplication of the metacarpals."

Mike pulled the lower part of the sheet back several inches. "Same with the metatarsals."

Muna rubbed her face. "I really need to wake up."

Oz reached over and pinched the back of her hand.

"Hey." She rubbed her hand. "What the...?"

Nash rumbled as she crossed her arms under her chest. "To show you it's not a dream."

Mike turned on his mechanical leg. "And because we don't hit women in the arm." He glanced back. "Like we have been doing for the last..." He frowned. "What day is this?"

Nash groused, "This is your third day being locked up in here since we took the gloves, boots, and helmet off."

Mike looked at Oz. "I need a nap."

Oz rolled his finger in the air.

Mike pointed at the X-ray. "We started here." Then he tapped the computer screen. "So we switched to electronic film and took X-rays of the entire body." He glanced back. "Better to know where you're going before you start."

After ensuring the locks on the wheels were set, Oz leaned against the other table. Nash could see the exhaustion in the older man. They had seen the two men leave late at night, but they never saw them come in the morning. Muna and Nash had assumed they came while the women were in the basement shooting or out to breakfast. Either way, it was a long day.

While Mike swiped through the slides, Oz explained how the braid of wires duplicated and secured the vital skeletal structure. "The distal digits have five wire braids, and then nine wires in the arms and eleven in the legs. The spine is about double but still semi-flexible."

"Flexible, but only as flexible as maybe the average forty-year-old man in reasonable shape and flexibility."

Muna snickered as she remembered a term she had learned during her time in the hospital in Colorado. "Flexible for a man who is all stoved up?"

Nash rumbled. "You mispronounced all blown up."

Muna rolled her hand and finger out in the air to point at Nash.

Oz nodded. "The term comes from a man looking like he's walking around with his legs stuffed into a metal stovepipe. It makes him walk stiffly." He turned to the body under the sheet. "But our eight ball here isn't so stiff. In fact, we had no problem flexing him out of the suit or making him do a sit-up. But matching a twenty-year-old on the balance beam...? Not going to happen."

"Eight ball?" Muna narrowed her eyes. "As in shooting pool?"

Oz rolled the body up on its side and raised the sheet to expose the right shoulder to the spine. The tattoo of the black pool ball had aged, but it hadn't turned green. "Exactly like shooting pool, Muna."

Nash watched her old instructor's face as she stepped over to the table and stooped to examine the tattoo. "Is this leather?"

Mike stretched his neck and hummed. "Let's say yes and leave it at that for right now."

Nash glanced up at the taciturn medical examiner. She peeked at a silent Oz and then gently lifted more of the sheet. The leather ended just above the lumbar region. The leather had tiny brass grommets set along the edge. Lacing attached the leather upper body to the canvas cloth of the lower body and hips. Nash slipped a finger into the lacing and pulled gently. The round braided nylon or silk lacing easily adjusted to the pull. Nash speculated that the purpose of it was to ensure the large joint of the hips could flex without causing any damage to the cloth or the leather. She straightened and studied her old instructor.

Oz shook his head. "No. We never even imagined something like this at the Body Farm. But it's ingenious, isn't it?"

"And creepy, as well." She glanced back at Muna, who was standing against the other examining table. Nash noticed the blanching of her knuckles. "Are you okay, Muna?"

The small woman slowly blinked. "I'll tell you in a few minutes."

"Do you want to sit down?"

Mike offered to get her a chair. She shook her head. "Just keep going. What else, Oz?"

Oz pulled the sheet back to expose the neck and shoulders. The neck flared, and there was a slight bump where the shoulders started. "We haven't cut it open, but the leather of the neck comes down and slips into what we think is like a leather flange of the shoulder. Something is going on here, as there is evidence of a hidden stitching line an inch back from the edge." He slapped one hand over the other. "A leather worker will make a shallow beveled cut in the leather. They can peel back the edge a quarter inch or so and stitch along in the bevel. After the stitching is done, they can glue the leather back over the stitching. This is called a hidden stitch. It's used on fine furniture, saddles, and in plastic surgery."

He gripped the head in the sheet and turned it. The neck slid around. Turning it back, he relaxed and let the body roll back onto the table—under the sheet.

Nash narrowed one eye to a slit. "How much of the body is leather?"

Mike swallowed. "Sixty-eight percent. Plus or minus a percent or two."

Nash moved her scrutiny. "Hands and feet?"

The man swallowed. "Leather to the elbows and knees. Then

they transition to the heavy cotton canvas, and then back to leather until the hips and shoulder joints."

Muna cleared her throat. "The head?"

Oz pointed at the body. "You saw it. It's leather."

"From what I saw through the helmet's visor... The face looked... um... reasonably human."

Oz peered at Mike.

Mike gently nodded; his eyes closed in a slow blink.

Oz blew out his breath through pursed lips. "What's your question?"

Muna's eyes narrowed as they bounced from Mike to Nash and back to Oz. She sagged against the table. She felt like she was back in his class at Quantico. "What kind of leather?"

"Human."

Nash shifted. "No doubt?"

Oz's head barely moved. "None."

"And tanned."

"All of it."

Nash watched Muna's knuckles turn lighter.

11

PUNCHING PAPER

POWDER SAT, patiently waiting for the poodle to finish acting out. The woman was as yappy as her dog as she barked at the tall woman dressed in an official FBI jacket. Nash showed her badge and tried to explain how her anti-terrorist K-9 was also trying to work and never used a leash. The woman and dyed pink poodle were having none of it and kept threatening to call the police. Nash offered to dial for the woman.

The mounted patrol heard the nonstop yap that wasn't going away and rode over. As they rode up, the two officers nodded. "Agent. Anything we can help with?"

The woman huffed and pulled her dog in tighter. "Oh, sure. Call friends of yours. A private citizen doesn't have a chance anymore. This city has gone to hell in a handbag." Exasperated, she picked up Jewels and stomped off.

The older officer held up his finger as his voice trailed off. "I think the word is hand… basket…"

The younger rolled her eyes. "FBI, if I'm not mistaken."

Nodding, Nash leaned and scratched Powder's head. "Nash. Nash Running Bear. And this is Powder."

The older officer turned back with a smile. "You work with Agent al-Faragi? We usually see her doing her runs at this time."

"She's punching paper today. She has her last Olympic qualifying shooting competition next week."

The two looked at each other and smiled. "We have a pool going at the station. Only the guy who was on vacation has the square where she doesn't make it to Paris."

"Yeah, I wouldn't bet against her. I've been shooting against her for too long."

The radio squawked too staticky for Nash to understand, but both officers rolled their eyes. "No restaurant for the weary."

Nash waved. "Stay safe."

The two horses turned, swishing their tails, and cantered down the trail.

Nash glanced at the shadows under the bushes. They were small and dark. Nash peeked at her watch. They had killed more than a few hours over a leisure breakfast followed by a long, distracted walk around Golden Gate Park. "I think we've gold-bricked enough. Let's go find your sister."

The cavernous office room was silent. Muna's desk was empty. Nash felt dirty for invading the other's space, but she pulled open the bottom drawer. The bag of guns was missing.

She sat on the desk she thought of as her West Coast desk and picked up the phone's handpiece. She missed the weight of a metal handpiece. It also made a satisfying sound when slammed down.

The voice sounded irritated and sharp. "Master."

"Lester, it's Nash. Is Muna still down there?"

"Define the word *still*. She shot her standard hundred rounds through all seven guns at four-thirty this morning. She came back at nine and demanded a stack of sniper targets and two full hundred-round slides of nines and fifties each. I tried to assign her an alley, but she breached the barrier and set up on the long range. She's been nesting on seven and six ever since."

Nash drew a deep breath through her nose. "The air-soft pistol and Olympic rifle?"

"Not yet. But she's shooting round robin with the nine-millimeter and the two fifties. She just drew her sixth slide of nines and fourth slide of fifties. No wadcutters. I'm getting worried. Even for someone yours and my size, that's a lot of abuse to the hand. I didn't notice a bloody glove, but I'm getting worried."

Nash looked at Powder lying under the windows in a slim slice of sunshine. "Stack four boxes of her Olympic ammo. Two and two. I'll be down in a minute. I'll need two boxes of nines."

"You want me to clip them for you?"

Nash thought about how fast she could go through twenty clips for her gun. "How many clips do you have for my nine?"

"Fifty."

She did want to think as she looked out the window. Less than a dozen little puffy clouds broke the solid blue of the sky. A line of darker blue reminded her of a distant past, of sitting on beaches, waiting for the next torture of training.

"Nash?"

She shook her head. "Sorry. Yeah, I'm here, Lester. Give me all fifty or whatever you have loaded."

"I'll put you on lane five. Whatever crap you two are working through, I don't wanna know, but Oz and Mike just came down a half hour ago. They camped on lanes one and three."

Nash grimaced. "Yeah. You don't want to know. I'll be down in a minute."

Walking to Powder, she ran her hand over the warm belly. "I'm going shooting with Muna and the boys. Are you okay here in the sun for a while?"

"I'll take her out if she needs it."

Nash twitched and looked over at the dark computer wall hiding the corner. Chips stood with a bowl in one hand and a spoon in the other. "What are you doing here?"

The blonde shrugged. "Mike called down yesterday and asked if

I could come to work on a special project. I don't think he trusted talking on the phone."

Nash stood. "What project?"

The young woman snorted and twitched her head toward the autopsy laboratory. "As nerdy as I am about computers and gaming, he and I talked in the past about my wanting to be an astronaut but never learned how to fly." She shoveled a small spoonful of cereal and fruit into her mouth. Chewing slowly and then swallowing, she smiled. "So he knew he had me at the word space suit." Her eyes grew wild as she pointed her spoon at the helmet, gloves, and boots. "How fucking amazeballs is that?"

Nash flexed her eyebrows as she shrugged her face. "Yeah. Amaze balls." She jerked her thumb over her shoulder. "Look... um..."

Chips nodded. "I heard. Go punch paper with Muna. The daddies are worried about her."

"Thanks. We'll talk later."

Nash paused at the triple-paned glass door. Glancing at the range master working with a speed loader to load more clips, she thought about some firefights she had in the sandbox. Only three people were shooting on the other side of the sound barrier, but it sounded like the worst Kandahar had produced.

Lester stuffed six more clips into the Styrofoam slide. Full, the slide would hold two hundred and forty rounds. He looked at Nash paused at the door. Glancing at the wall of the insulating windows, he grimaced. "Nonstop."

Nash sighed. Pulling her earmuffs off her neck and seated them on her head, she pushed through the door. The sound of the nines and fifty washed through the opening and then subsided as the door closed.

At alley five, Nash smiled at the sniper target. The replacement stack sat on the counter to her left. Drawing her weapon, she dropped out her service load and ejected the one in the barrel. She studied the rack of clips and then turned it around. The first clip flowed into her pistol, with the up movement countered by the down movement of cupping her grip and thumbing the release. As the slide of the weapon hit the front, her finger began squeezing off shots.

Empty, the clip dropped as her left hand replaced it with a full clip and slapped the slide back to cup her grip. The crosshair in the lower left corner disappeared right before the upper left.

The clip dropped, and then the X in the center disappeared, followed by the surrounding ring. Two shots under the left clip set the target to swing. Two more dropped the target from the right clip. The clip dropped as her hand hit the red recall button. She slid the fresh clip in. Clipped up the next target and hit the send button.

Pulling the slide, she raised the pistol and shot out the center as the target continued to its appointed destination. The next clip tore out the upper crosshairs. The next clip cut the target in half.

Old feelings, long-smoldering from a lifetime ago, surfaced and then dissolved in a nonstop flow of lead. Corners disappeared. Centers became vacant holes. The cardstock was no match for the onslaught.

And then the larger target appeared to her right.

The center red turned blank black as the paper emptied into the air. The target drew back, and a new target replaced it at the end of the thirty yards. It waved back one last time before the lower right corner twitched from the rapid-fire tearing away the crosshair. As the corner tore off, the left began to twitch and dance.

Nash continued her dance toward purge and redemption.

———

"I HEARD THE GIRLS INVADED A REAL BEACH, AND CHEF put on a barbecue." The early evening at Chow Fats was busy enough to provide an ambiance of being ignored for eating like Americans with no place to rush off to but muted enough to have a softer conversation if needed.

Chips set her bowl down and placed her chopsticks on the small stone pillow. "Frank took Ming and Tree down to Crystal Cove to see what it would be like eating on the sand." Her eyes rolled in a smirk. "Ming swears she is still finding sand where the sun doesn't shine. So they chartered a yacht to leisurely cruise along the coast while Chef stuffed them silly."

Muna frowned at Nash and then at Chips. "You didn't go with them?"

Chips laughed. "Oh, hell no. Eat on a rocking boat. No way. While they snuck off to sea, we were rocking the pinball world in San Diego. There's an exhibition hall in Balboa Park with nothing but old-school pinballs. No electronics. And best of all, Slug's initials weren't anywhere on the high score on any of the machines."

Muna snorted. "Are they now?"

The woman coyly smiled as she dragged out the word, "May... be..."

Nash looked at the side of her eyes as she thought. "Would there be any marked Chips?"

"Nope. CHP and PTE. It turns out Slug sucks at the old-school steel ball."

Muna rested her head against the booth as she smiled. "But you and Petey rock."

"So it says." She picked at the dim sum. "So, a lot of shooting today..."

Muna sobered. "Is that a question... or a statement?"

Chips' finger froze on the last crab dumpling. "Both?"

"The last qualifying competition is next week."

Chips slurped the crab dumpling and chewed as she bobbed her head. "Jazz said she got tickets. She and her Coast Guard friend are going out to watch."

Muna groaned. "Oh, yay. No pressure there."

Nash glared at the smaller agent. "Mina can always fly your folks down..."

Muna rubbed her middle finger along the side of her nose. "That would be just marvy."

Chips looked at Muna as her mouth opened. Nash jumped in. "Leave it. It's a long story. So, did Mike fill you in completely?"

"As complete as he could. They're still trying to pull some decent fingerprints off the hands. It would at least help give us directions toward who the person was. But I don't think the ridges would have survived the tanning." She jabbed the back of her chopsticks at Muna. "Even your super wiz-bang scanner and 3-D printer didn't help this time." Shrugging, she picked up the last half of an egg roll. "What do we know about where they found him?"

Nash raised her one finger off the table. "The report is sketchy at best." She rocked her head from shoulder to shoulder. "Ghost town. Two kids broke into the saloon. Found the astronaut had crashed through the roof and ceiling and landed on a table and chairs. Kind of the setup for a comedy skit on Saturday night."

Chips rolled her head, stretching her neck. "When are you going out to...?"

Nash parked her eyes in their upper left corners. "Yah-Ta-Hey. It's an actual place in New Mexico. I'll go while she's shooting."

Chips smirked. "Yeah. I know the place. It's below Ship Rock and north of Gallup. It's where the Southern Ute reservation meets the Navajo. The old trading grounds are there. Yah-Ta-Hey is the common greeting for the Ute and the Navajo, but it means *like a devil*. It's kind of like the old greeting of *Look what the cat dragged in*. Something my dad used to say."

Nash looked at her out of the side of her eye.

The girl laughed as she held up her hands in a shrug. "Hey. I got bored in Pueblo... so I drove around. First on Google Earth and then for real. You learn a lot of stuff by talking to old people. They love telling the young'uns all about the world."

12

THE DEVIL YOU KNOW

THE ROUGH GRAY wooden picnic table reminded Nash of similar tables from her childhood and military bases. The cross legs and five or six boards for a top seemed universal. In the sandbox, someone had burned a sign into the wood. *Brought to you from your folk's backyard.*

Powder sat next to her as they shared the burritos. The rest area was little more than four parking spaces off the highway, fronting two picnic tables, looking across the desert.

Nobody had splurged any paint or stain on the table or benches. The splurge was the chains running through the top of the crossed legs bolted to the concrete. Nash chuckled at the three-inch bolt pulled from the concrete. Nobody cared, and it hung from the end of the chain. Who was going to steal it? Who needed a matching set of picnic tables behind their shack?

She held out the last quarter of the second burrito. "You might as well have this. I think I've had enough beans." Powder stared at her as if to ask if she was feeling okay. "Go ahead. Your farts won't be any worse than mine."

Powder delicately took the offered food and set it on the table.

She peered around at the barren landscape and finally wolfed it down.

Nash burped a laugh. "Couldn't find any coyotes to share with?" She ruffled Powder's ears and head as the dog licked her lips and leaned over to touch her nose to Nash's cheek. "Yeah, I love these times as well."

They sat quietly, watching the lack of movement across the miles of course sand, rocks, and the occasional bush or cacti. With the calm, Nash could feel her heart rate and blood pressure lower. The desert heat felt like hanging her feet in Bone Creek. It was a form of going home. She had first realized the feeling on the side of a mountain in Afghanistan. The quieting, the calm, and the warmth. At least here she felt assured nobody would shoot at her.

She twitched and scanned again. Desert. Not even a coyote or roadrunner. The desert hadn't changed. Not even another car on the highway. *That's what I get for taking the back roads.* But her senses had changed. Something was different. Not bad... just... different.

Nash crumpled up the burrito's wrapping papers. "It's time to go. We're burning daylight."

The garage monkey smiled when she asked to see the engine. He had joked she was afraid of getting a straight six or even the V-6 engine. He pointed out the larger engine identifications. His laugh was deep when she explained about her experiences with and owning a 700HP Hell Cat. He had patted the white 300 and explained it was his only muscle car they had left and how he didn't want to lose it in the Badlands of Colorado. *Word gets around.*

THE DEPUTY STATION WAS LITTLE MORE THAN TWO windows and a door. Not the smallest Nash had seen, but more than she had expected. As the glass-paneled door swung open, she half expected it to hit a set of tinkling bells. Powder led her into the cooler air conditioning. It wasn't the cold she had walked into in other areas, but it did temper the heat of the day. The man leaning with one elbow on the counter dipped his head as she closed the door.

Nash pulled out her identification wallet. "I'm FBI Agent Nash Running Bear."

He peeked down and waved his finger from his unmoving hand. "Saw the badge on your dog. What can we do for you?" His voice and behavior weren't snippy, gruff, or arrogant, just not inviting.

Nash figured he got minimum small talk during the day. "We're looking for a deputy, Yazzie Zapata?"

"Yazzie is the last name. Zapata is the first."

Nash leaned in. "Oh. Sorry. My uncle's first name is Yazzie." She stopped and stared at Powder in thought. "Or maybe his last name..." She looked up and shrugged. "He's just Uncle to me and everyone else."

"What can I do for you?"

Nash looked for a nameplate most law enforcement wore. Seeing none, she realized she stood in the entire substation. It is big enough for one deputy and a tight squeeze for two. "I'm here concerning the astronaut you found up the road a piece." She hoped she sounded local enough for him to loosen up a notch or two on his personality belt.

He didn't move, but his face darkened, and she could see his jaw tighten. "Why?"

She leaned in closer. "Because I'm the Federal Bureau of Investigation. It's what we do. We investigate. Now, do I get cooperation, or does my dog need to find that for you?"

His eyes twitched. "What does your dog do?"

Nash paused and then leaned in with a half-smirk. "She finds drugs, explosives, where bodies are buried, and better places to bury new ones. And on Wednesdays, she finds where certain people are hiding their balls so she can destroy them. Any more questions, or can we get to it?"

He quietly cleared his throat and swallowed. "What do you need to do?"

Nash blinked in acknowledgment of her win and eased back an inch. She watched the man's second swallow—it was slower but deeper. "How about we just go over the sketchy report first? You were the first on the scene?"

His head twitched. "No. A couple of kids broke into the old saloon. Maybe to see if there was anything they could steal."

"And they found the body, so they called you. This place is how far away?"

He straightened for the first time. Nash watched for stiffness to explain his non-movement and shorthand speech. He sighed. "About an hour. If you know where it is."

Nash was tired of the blank wall of nothing. "Look. Maybe we got off on the wrong foot here. How about we shake and start over?" She stuck her hand to the midway point of the counter. The man recoiled as if she had just dropped a rattlesnake on the counter.

Both of his hands folded up at his chest as he leaned away. "I don't touch people." His voice was a flat statement instead of one of horror.

Nash's eyes narrowed. "Because then you would know something about them? Or the voices?"

His eyes turned to slits. His voice trailed into a breath. "What do you know… about…?"

Nash opened her eyes and shrugged her face and one shoulder. "My folks have been dead for a long time. But they are both only a close of my eyes away. My dog is the same. I don't know what she sees or hears, but I never question her response."

He didn't relax as much as his guard moved closer to dropping. "What do they say to you?"

She shrugged and pushed out her lower lip. "You know parents. You need to get serious, stop running all over the place, and settle down. The usual stuff they never had time to tell me in life. You?"

He sighed and glanced over his shoulder as his thumbs hooked into his pants pockets. "My mother was Ute. I never learned Ute; I only speak Navajo. So she yammers at me, but I don't understand."

"Have you tried talking to her in English?"

His eyes drooped into his shaking head. "She hated the white man. When I was five or six, she made me go to the store and buy what we needed from the white family at the trading post."

"Maybe it's time to learn, Ute? Make peace with your mother. I'd think it would make her proud you were at least trying. What about your father?"

The man sat on the edge of the desk behind him. "He's Navajo. He says if his ex-wife is talking to me across the great desert, it's my problem. Dad doesn't want to hear about her. He remarried twenty years ago and doesn't want to have my mother's spirit in his home."

Nash bobbed her head softly. The man was stuck in a complicated life she understood but had few answers for her life as it was. "Getting back to the astronaut. Who put him in the bag and thought to use an airfreight container?"

He raised his hand to chest height and then stuck the thumb back in his black uniform pants. "The bags are what we use for large drug busts... well... if we had any. We have a bunch of stuff the federal government gives us, but we don't have a need. We need newer four-wheel-drive units. Or I should say, we could use more of that kind of help. They pass out leftover stuff from the war in the Middle East, but we have no use for a big truck called a rat."

Nash smiled softly. "It's called an MRAP. Basically, it's an armored personal carrier on steroids. They invented it for us to survive IEDs. But it would suck in a high-speed car chase. I think a moped or a kid on a bicycle could outrun it. But the shipping container?"

"We knew we had to ship it somewhere. I called Alaska Airlines and explained what I needed to do, and the next day, there was a guy out front with a truck and a forklift on the back. We took some deputies out to the ghost town, bagged the spaceman, and stuck him in the container. Alaska signed for what I hoped was the end."

Nash snorted. "Until I showed up."

"Until you showed up."

Powder leaned against her leg. Nash peered down at the head, looking through the counter at the man the dog couldn't see. She leaned and stroked in front of one ear with a single finger. Her voice was only for Powder. "Okay. We make nice, nice."

Nash straightened and studied the deputy. The all-black pants and shirt didn't fit in her idea of ideal clothing to wear in the heat of New Mexico. But then, the mix of land of Indian enchantment, Mexican food, and white man laws made just as much sense. "Is there phone service out at the ghost town?"

The deputy twitched. The question isn't what he had expected. "Um… yeah. I think it was two or three bars, but the nearest cell is probably out on the highway somewhere near Naschitti. Why?"

Nash glanced around at the front door and then back. Her braid responded to the quick snap and circled onto her chest, and the weight pulled it the rest of the way. "I figured either you're coming with me, or you can give me the GPS coordinates, and I go alone."

"What about your dog?"

Nash blinked at someone taking things so literally. "I'll leave her here. I haven't fed her in two days. She'd probably finish your scrawny body by the time I get back." She gave him the famous Mina Deadpan face when facing heads of Congress.

He blinked a few times. "My cruiser isn't… there's no room. I mean, there's a computer…"

Nash nodded. "I know what you mean. We'll take my car. There's plenty of room for us in the back. We'll let the dog do the driving."

He blinked in confusion through his nine types of frowning. Finally, his face lit up. "Oh. You made a joke."

Nash carefully lowered and then raised her head. "Yes. It's what we call a joke. It's a form of teasing. The FBI trains us to deploy the tactic when someone is taking all this too seriously."

His hand slowly escaped the crossed arms from his chest. He pointed at her. "Good tactic to know."

13

DESERT WALK

THE MAN HAD SPOKEN ONLY the seventeen needed words of direction to get them out of town and headed up Highway 491. As the houses disappeared, their sparsity became replaced by stunted sagebrush. Nash stopped looking at the bushes when she realized she would have to bend over to harvest less than a meager handful of leaves.

Nash reached behind her to feel the air vents at the back of the console. The flow was not what was spewing from the dash, but Powder wasn't panting. But a glance confirmed she wasn't sleeping either. The man was an unknown.

"Does the sage smell if you harvest the leaves?"

The man shrugged. "I never touch the plants."

Nash snuck a peek. "Because they might talk to you also?"

He scowled at her. "No. Because I don't like getting dirty. I never did."

"Even when you were growing up? No running around in the desert? No playing with cars and trucks in the dirt? What kind of childhood did you have?"

He looked out the side window. "I stayed in my room and read. Or rode my bike to the library."

Nash studied the man for a moment. "You don't look like you're out of shape. How did you pass the police qualifications?"

"There's a gym in the apartment building. I work out. Mostly at night, when nobody is around."

"On equipment other people have been touching and sweating on?"

He spat a small laugh. "I know what you're trying to do. No. I wipe everything down with Sani wipes. They may only kill ninety-nine point nine percent of the other people. But everything smells clean." He shrugged and glanced back at Powder. "How often do you wash your dog?"

Nash smiled at the tit-for-tat she hadn't gotten since the Corps. "She showers with me. If I'm dirty, she's dirty. If I'm wet, she's wet. We're more of a team than most other K-9 teams."

"Where does she sleep?"

Nash sighed as she weighed what to tell this stranger. "With a rough night of terrors, we're both in the living room. Otherwise, she's on our bed. Either between us or at the foot if it's too hot."

"You're married."

"Yes."

"Oh."

The desert slid past. The few buildings vibrated in the mirror as Nash realized they had just driven past Yah-Ta-Hey. She didn't notice any place she could buy a trinket for Uncle. She still thought the greeting was something the white man made up for the movies. But the GPS, as a white man machine, said it's a place.

She glanced over at the man as she checked the side mirror. "When did your mother start talking to you?"

He jerked as if she had touched him with a cattle prod or a taser set on a low setting. His breathing raced for a few pants and then settled back. "At her funeral."

Nash rocked with understanding. "You could hear her? Or you only thought she was talking to you?"

"She was sitting next to me. It was very unsettling. I don't think she liked the minister the funeral home had hired."

"And she only spoke Ute?"

He drew in a breath through his nose and watched the desert. "Mostly. I kind of understood what she was complaining about. She thought the service was a waste of money and time. None of her friends were there. Shock. I didn't even know she had friends."

Nash cleared the mirrors and watched the truck in the rearview mirror turn off. She hadn't noticed a road. "What does she talk about now?"

He peeked over. "If I understand her, it's about my not being married and giving her grandbabies. It's the same old story. But it doesn't matter. What is she going to do if I produce a baby? Hold them? How?"

Nash shrugged her shoulder and looked over with a soft smile. "Parents. Go figure. I think mine gave up years ago. My sister isn't even married, and I don't think she'll ever even date, much less get married to procreate."

"Does she hate men?"

Nash shrugged. "I do not know. I think it's more like she doesn't like personal interaction. She's set in her ways the same as she was twenty-five years ago. Her only phone is the green one we had as kids on the kitchen counter—she's not old enough to remember the black metal one. She reads what she has to, and that is the extent of her wanting to gather anything new."

"What does she do on her computer?"

Nash's head negated the idea of anything other than the last century. "And you've never learned Ute...?"

"The nuns wouldn't let us speak anything tribal. Speaking anything but English would get you a ruler on your hands or a mesquite stick to your behind. Better to just speak English."

Nash glanced at his finger, waving left and a sign on the right. "Just before Naschitti, we turn left. I get enough Navajo here and there, so I'm making up for it now."

"I thought nuns and corporal punishment were only horror stories from the past."

He shrugged. "My past. I guess when they became a problem somewhere more progressive, they sent them off to teach in Indian schools."

"So you went to a parochial school? Why not a public school?"

The man scratched the back of his head. "It was the public school. The two sisters were the only nuns. But they even scared the shorts off the gym teachers. And if the two of them went on the warpath, not even a parent would go near the school. Kids today have it easy. Their teachers are teaching off their student debt. After spending five years in the pueblos, they wipe out all the federal debt. Same for my doctor. But she's going to stay. She says the occasional coyote in her backyard is better than the guns and drugs in the project slums she grew up in."

"But your mother still visits you? How often?"

His face tiredly sagged as he looked over. "When I get close. Like now. I've heard her talk the last few miles. The closer I get to Ship Rock, the stronger her voice."

Nash frowned as she glanced over. "What is she saying?"

"I don't know. Like I can hear her talking to someone, but in the next apartment. The walls are thin, but it's too muffled to understand."

"But you know it's Ute."

"It's all she would talk."

Nash twisted her head slightly. "But you understood her at her funeral?"

"She always spoke—a mix. Some Ute, some Navajo, and mostly English because she knew it was all I really understood. She might be upset with me, but she's still a mother." He pointed toward the small dirt road ahead. "Take it slow. I don't know if the sand has turned soft or not."

The SUV eased off the highway onto the hard-packed dirt road.

The center looked soft, but the two tracks held firm. Nash peeked over. "How far?"

"A few miles. We turn right after the turtle rock."

"But you understood what she was saying." Nash peeked out of the side of her eyes. "She wasn't forcing Ute on you?"

He shook his head. "She gave up when I got into high school. I found a photo of a girl—blond with piercing blue eyes. The smile was more a question than happiness. I guess that's why they used it for the picture frames the drugstore sold—like the Mona Lisa chick. But I was tired of the questions and nagging in a language I didn't understand or wanted to learn. I had reached my breaking point. So I thumb-tacked the photo to the wall over my bed."

Nash's head snapped back to the man. "Like she was your girlfriend?"

He shrugged into a coy look out the side window. His voice dropped—a soft tone of shame. "She never asked." But he knew he had crossed the line. "I left it there when I left for Arizona State."

Nash nodded. "Anything but tribe." She understood the sentiment.

The rock was a large, flat-faced boulder with a brown crust that only came after millions of years of exposure to the weather in the desert. At a man's head height, someone had carved a petroglyph of a turtle past the crust to the soft gray stone below. Much larger was a spray-painted graffiti bomb of a popular group of teenage turtles. On the sand in front stood a herd of concrete yard statues. Some were painted natural colors, some with faded psychedelic color schemes, and others just raw concrete. Nash smiled at something her sergeant had once said about watching a nomad encampment pack and leave in the early hours before the sun was up and burning. *Off like a herd of turtles—baling out.* It was years later she had learned a group of turtles was called a bale.

"That's a lot of respect or homage. It reminds me of some shrines I've seen around the world." Nash eased the SUV onto the smaller track leading into a canyon.

The deputy rocked as his head swiveled, watching the collective. "I don't remember what came first, Michaelangelo and friends or some statues. I think the ninjas were a seventies or eighties thing. But some of those turtles look like the Beatle's album about the yellow submarine."

Nash smirked softly as the hills closed in to form the canyon. "I think you're off by a bit. The Beatle's heyday was the wild sixties. Like the summer of love was in sixty-eight, but people confuse it with the sexual revolution, which was more in the middle of the seventies."

He waved his hand in the air. "And then HIV and AIDS brought all that to a screaming halt, so people just focused on their careers."

Nash snorted. "And then teachers, who were still confused or angry because they had missed all the fun, taught us the confusing history we were supposed to learn in school. We made more sense of it than some of them did."

As they rounded a knee of the mountain, the small valley widened and spread out. The low, weathered hills framed the interior in a guarded shadowbox of sandstone and spilling decomposition.

Centered in the expansive valley. The abandoned ghost town stood, frozen in time. Dilapidated buildings and boarded-over windows spoke of a once-thriving community now left to decay. The silence deafened save the imagined occasional old wood creaking or rustling of non-existing leaves in a remembered breeze, like a keyhole image of a forgotten world, a glimpse into a past, begging exploration.

Nash felt Powder's body heat on her arm, more than she heard the dog move. Powder was fully alert and in silent mode. Their four eyes danced about the buildings. Even through the closed windows and over the air conditioning, the acrid scent of sunbaked creosote stung the back of Nash's nose.

The car rolled to a stop as they surveyed the town from a distance.

Memories of visiting her father at the railroad yards with its stacks of blackened wood sleepers churned up. The railroads had always struggled with replacing the rail beds from the eighteen hundreds—made of untreated sleepers. Those sleepers didn't last long before they started rotting, which could lead to derailments. With the turn of the century and the oil boom, creosote was used to preserve the timbers. But, as her father pointed out, they only soaked timbers in the preservative, which only penetrated so deep. American engineers only realized the benefits of pressure treating after seeing Europe's well-preserved railroads. So they forcefully pushed the corrosive oil deeper and replaced the old, soaked creosote. Now the replacement uses even more caustic and dangerous chemicals.

The town's builders painted the wooden siding with creosote to prevent rot and turn any rain. The intense sunshine carried its own threat but only baked the raw oil deeper into the wood. They painted any other adornment sparingly.

Nash twitched her head toward the deputy. "How much do you know about this town?"

"Not much. It's always been here. Kids come out and have parties... you saw the turtles..."

She studied the hills and the sun-grayed steeple of the white-washed church at the other end of the town. Only a few buildings along the overly wide main street boasted rails to tie up a horse. The missing fascinated her most. *No watering troughs. Where do the horses drink?* "There might be ghosts here... but this is no ghost town."

14

IT GOES WHERE?

1958 CHRISTMAS

THE FUR on the polar bear glistened under the lights of the one hundred tiny lightbulbs and the four thousand pendent crystals in the chandelier. A crystal chandelier hung ten feet above the standing bear's head. The ceiling, painted to match the dome in Versailles, hovered fifteen feet higher. The dais supporting the stuffed bear added two feet and weighed over eight hundred pounds. Betty was proud of the steel spine work she had devised to resist even the most ardent drunk a Hollywood party could produce. But she still felt the urge to brush the fur one more time.

"Admiring your work, Miss Dorfman? I did get the name right, didn't I? It is still Dorfman?"

Betty turned gently to the voice as she adjusted what she called her Hollywood face. The smile was soft, but the lips didn't part to show her teeth. She knew they were anything but Hollywood. "No, Mister Magnuson, I was admiring how beautiful the lighting was to show off your new trophy." She waved her outstretched hand at the voluminous foyer. "The Carrera marble of the walls and floor perfectly convey the aura of the icebergs and snow." She took his hand. "So good to see you again, and what a wonderful surprise to be invited to the premier party of the season. Thank you for this."

He bowed and kissed the back of her hand. "I don't know why we have ever denied ourselves of your radiant ambiance. So good to have you come. Was Will able to accompany you?"

Her left hand, missing the small finger and most of a thumb, pulled at the side of her dark blue velvet dress as she curtsied. As she straightened, the hand wound into the extra fabric to hide the deformity. "No. He wasn't feeling well and stayed home. He's been working too many hours lately on a special project, and I'm afraid it has affected his health. I worry about him."

"Well, give him my best and tell him to look after his health as much as he looks after his business." He pointed at the large archway into the next room. "I heard Jerry brought a nice string ensemble to play in the ballroom. And the caterer said he would have some of those little shrimp puffy things that were all the rage at Cannes this year. So enjoy. We'll talk later."

The man wandered off in a cloud of smoke to press his cigar-laden hand to everyone else's hands. Betty slowly shook her head as she looked up at the polar bear towering twelve feet above her. She patted his foot one last time. "Goodbye Nanook. It was fun while it lasted." She knew she could never tell a soul how the body had come from the Pittsburg Zoo, not from the barren reaches of the far north. The beast had lived out his long-imprisoned life in content. His passing was peaceful in his sleep, not at the hands of a hunt.

The music did sound wonderful.

THE LARGE WALRUS MUSTACHE COCKED AT AN ANGLE AS Will pulled the skin over the semi-soft form. This form would take thousands of blows, deform, and then snap back decade after decade. He looked at the face and made adjustments before gluing the final attachments around the eyes. "We had some strange requests over the years, my friend. The child's pet mouse, the family dog or cat, and even Roy's horse. But this, my friend, you topped them all. But I understand why, and thank you."

The soft light in the windows set high on the walls spilled muted onto the back alley. A cat scurried along the wall, stopped, and sniffed at the small wad of curiosity, and then continued walking. There was no sense of what Christmas Eve meant. There was no special item to eat, no toy to play with, no warm fireside to curl up next to.

THE FESTIVITIES ROARED ON IN TRUE HOLLYWOOD fashion. But glitz and glamour weren't Betty's cup of tea. She squinted at the glow of a rising sun over the San Gabriel Mountains —Christmas day. All she wanted was to find her way back to her bed.

The office was a pastiche of understated wealth and power, with plush carpets, luxurious leather furnishings, and dark wood accents. The side chairs could easily accommodate giants or shrink regular-sized men. As Betty made note of the intimidating desk chair, she couldn't help but imagine how small she would appear compared with the cigar-wielding head honcho of Burbank Studios who sat there.

"What's this about Mister Magnuson?"

He held his hand without the cigar, thankfully, toward the easy chair. "Please. Reggie. We're going to be business partners, so let's at least act like friends."

Betty gently eased her knees to bend and sat. "Okay... Reggie. Please explain the part about being in business. And I must say, it sounds more like something the tiger would tell the chicken."

"Well, Valentine made me an unusual business deal at the first of the year." He leaned back, collecting his thoughts.

Betty straightened her dress over her knees so it hid instead of revealing the braces. "What sort of offer?"

He held up his hand in a stop sign. He swallowed. "You know about the dummies?"

Her eyes dipped. "Yes. We made them. I laced every single one of them. We sent all seven to you back in September."

His head bobbed gracefully. "Yes. And they are exquisite. Every single one of them. The finish is fantastic. The stitching is exceptional..."

She lowered one eyelid as she looked at him with her head cocked to the other side. "I hear a but coming."

"The contract was for eight."

She shrugged. "Give us a month. We'll make another one. I'll even do you one better. How about I send you two instead?"

He held his hand up again. "I'm fine. Valentine didn't expect the eighth one to finish before the hiatus. So it's right on schedule. In fact, I suspect your father's working tonight. But the dummy's not what I need to talk to you about."

"Then what?"

He adjusted in the chair as he cleared his throat. "I don't want to sound rude or be offensive, but business deals tend not to have any sensitivities. Money doesn't understand privacy or have personal feelings..."

She straightened as she clutched her small purse with both hands. "I'm not a child... Reggie."

He held out his hand and then waved her down. His hand rolled over, pointing at her knees. "How's your health? The doctor's bills... they covered?"

"Does this have anything to do with our business?"

He nodded a single nod. "Your father... he's how old now?"

"Seventy-two. And you warned me you were going to be brutish, but all this personal information is important. Why?"

"Please. A little more leeway and I'll explain everything. So he can work for a few more years… and then what? Can you sell the business?"

She studied the man as she thought. Her days were about keeping the animals clean and sellable, not about selling the business. Or, what happens after her father can't or doesn't work anymore? Five or ten years seems like a lifetime away until it isn't. "I can't imagine anyone buying it. It would be more of someone to just take the key. But the building is worth something. But I don't even want to think about what to do with all the animals. I'm sure some museums might want a few of the animals for their natural history wings… but… beyond that…"

Reggie laid the cigar backward on the edge of the side table and turned back. "And you live in…?"

"I rent an apartment three blocks from the shop. But I think you already know about my living arrangements. Didn't you."

"Yes, I did. Sorry, but I've had to research much of what Valentine included in our deal."

"Which you still haven't gotten around to saying…"

Reggie fished the inner pocket of his jacket and pulled out a piece of paper. "Here's a copy of Valentine's last will and testament. I'm one witness on the original, so even though the state can force me to adjudicate the letter and intent of his will, it wouldn't matter —I'm a willing participant. And as you know, Melba and I never had children. So even after the studio and I are separated, my estate will still honor and carry out the extent of this will."

Betty read the will. It was short and simple. But it covered the rest of her life. Her hand and the paper floated gently back to her lap. "I don't understand."

"After the war, your father took Valentine under his wing. You two make his only family. He had little, but what he had, he wanted it to provide for you after he and your father passed or couldn't provide for you. As for the taxidermy? When it's time, the studio will pay you the going rate for the business, lock, stock, and bear, or falcon, as it were. When the building's empty, I'll help you find a buyer who will pay top dollar. Burbank's up-and-coming, and the downtown is becoming valuable. That, you'll put away in a bank for anything you need or want down the road. But the house…" He pointed at the piece of paper. "Is yours to live in as long as you want or the rest of your life. It's rent and maintenance-free. They all belong to the studio. And I'm sure we can even cover a phone. Just don't call New York or Paris all the time."

She picked up the paper and studied it. "But it says here…"

He bowed his head. "You've been on the studio's medical plan since October. We just haven't gotten around to telling you until now. I tried to speak to you after Valentine's funeral… but…"

"It was not an easy time."

He rocked in understanding. "I hate to spoil your Christmas like this, but I wanted to make sure you started the new year with an understanding. And you can call me at any time if you have questions. Or need anything. I'm always at the office or here. Either can take a message or find me." He smiled. "You can think of me as your Daddy Warbucks."

She looked up from the paper. "I never read the book."

His eyes shot up. "The movie? Shirley Temple?"

Her head vibrated. "I've never been to the movies."

He smiled. "Under the ballroom is another room. We'll have you over anytime you want to see a movie. You tell me what movie you want to watch, and I'll get it. We can even make popcorn."

"Popcorn?"

His face looked crushed. "You've never had popcorn?"

"Of course I have. But you said you could even make popcorn…"

He leaned back, laughing. "You put it in a bag, and then you can eat it while you watch a movie. Oh, Saturday nights are going to be grand around here."

15

IF IT WALKS LIKE A DUCK

NASH STROLLED in the middle of the street. The creosote stench had subsided, or she had gotten used to it. Behind her orange mirrored aviators, her eyes jumped from the hitching post to the boardwalk, to each window or doorway. She evaluated and cataloged each piece of wood. None of the construction matched the heavy timbers her father had built their expansive front porch from. But then, few people had access to the waste pile of the railcar liners he sifted through over the years. He chuckled about what the white man corporation didn't pay the Indian in money; they made up by helping him build his home and heat it during the winter. Knowing where fresh roadkill was lying still warm helped fill the freezer or jerky bin.

She paused and looked at the buildings. The bank was across the street from the jail. The land office was between the bank and the saloon. Starting the street stood the blacksmith, horse boarding, and corral. Turning to the other end of the street, squatted the church with a faded try at whitewash. *Dry goods store?* She turned from the saloon and toward exactly where she expected had sat the Drover's Dry Goods.

Her right boot scraped at the dirt of the street. It sounded more like light gravel on the side of a standard street or dirt on a marching field. She realized what was wrong was the street. Trails in Harkin County, boot camp, Buds, and Afghanistan all had a softness to them. This street had none of those.

Kneeling, she looked along the street and from side to side. There were no ruts, as well as no crowning. The street was flat as the explanation. This wasn't a dirt street. She dug her finger at the surface. She penetrated as deep as her tight-trimmed fingernail. "Explain to me again how old this ghost town is?" She pivoted to look over at the man sitting on the edge of the raised wooden walkway.

He shrugged. "There were a lot of new towns in the middle of the eighteen hundreds. Socorro, Lincoln, and even Las Vegas became cities before the Civil War. But Taos and Sante Fe were already a hundred years old. But with the wild west and the white man running cattle and shooting each other... there were a lot of little boomtowns all over the West. Why?"

She pointed past the church. "Where does the valley lead?"

He glanced northwest where she was pointing. "Nowhere. It's a box canyon. It stops about a half mile further on."

Nash smirked. "So a cattle driver would drive their cattle in here, only to have to drive them back out the way they came? So what did they mine around here?"

"Nothing here. Silver and gold are mostly down south of ABQ. Up here, you'd be driving your cattle up the trace to Pueblo or cut west to the high line over near Mesa Grande into Mormon country."

Nash stood. Folding back each finger as she enumerated. "No cattle because they drove them out there near the highway. No mining because those mines were a hundred miles away. That leaves only the saloon, the whorehouse, and other assorted tourism. As we all know, a horny cowboy will ride days for a shot of whiskey and to jump in bed with a piece of fluff." She turned and pointed at the land office. "But we need a business office to manage all the land sales?"

"What are you saying, Agent?"

"You got a knife?"

"Sure…"

She pointed at the street as she swept the dirt back and forth with her boot. "I want you to dig a bit into the dirt here."

He stood with a hurt look on his face. "Why?"

She studied him. He wasn't the golden boy of the department. He'd been beaten and shoved to the bottom too many times. "Humor me, deputy. I have a mystery I need help to solve. But first, I need a hole about six inches deep, and I don't have a knife."

He walked over cautiously and kneeled. Pulling out his pocketknife, he stuck it in the dirt. It got as far as Nash's finger had. "Hard packed."

"Keep trying."

He cut at the dirt and then stabbed. After a few minutes, he had turned over a hole too small to lay his little finger in. "Like trying to dig up the asphalt in front of the substation. Maybe harder."

Nash bobbed her head as she looked down at him. "You can stop digging now."

He looked up with a question on his face. "But you said…?"

"Yeah. I know." She pointed with her hand flat along the street. "While you're down low, look at the street. What do you notice the most?"

He looked both ways. Picking up the small stone he had loosened from the street, he bounced it in his hand. "Flat." He peeked up. "Too flat?"

She dipped her head to one side. "Too flat. And hard as an asphalt street. This town didn't exist in 1863 or even 1920. They built this town for another reason, and nobody lived here." She waved at the buildings. "Not the banker, the sheriff, and not even the land office owner. I'll bet there was never any liquor or even whores in the saloon. Come on. I want to see where you found the astronaut."

Zap slipped his knife down the slit between the two doors. The bolt slid back, and the door swung in. He held his hand out to Nash, but Powder stepped in and stopped. Nash held her hand out to Zap's chest. "Not until she gives us the okay."

A minute later, Powder returned to the door, looked up, and turned back into the saloon.

Zap shrugged at Nash. "Now?"

"Now."

Nash pushed the door open and evaluated the classic barroom. She hadn't watched a lot of Western movies, but the barrooms all seemed to be the same... or the reverse. The bar had shelves for the bottles that were too high to reach. A large mirror graced the center of the back wall where the bartender could watch with his back to the room. But, with this room, there was too much room between the tables. Her old squad, two abreast, could wind their way to the bar and touch no one sitting at the tables.

She ticked her chin at Zap. "Where was the astronaut?"

Waving his hand left, he turned. "In the other room."

Nash studied the gaping hole in the ceiling and roof. The crushed table was directly below as if planned. "How did you get the astronaut into the bag and then the container?" She stepped in and moved a few chunks of lathe and plaster. The thin boards looked like they had been bent over a knee to break or cleaner. The plaster showed no signs of adhering to the boards; it only formed over the boards. She pulled out a stick and held it to her face, studying the surfaces.

The deputy rocked from boot to boot. "There were four of us. The other guys wanted a chance to get paid to see the town."

She peered at the nervous man as she held the stick out. "What's wrong with the break? More importantly, what's wrong with the stick?"

He examined both sides and the ends. He shrugged and offered it back.

Nash's eyes slid shut. "What's wrong with the break?"

He shrugged again. "It's broken."

Nash grabbed the stick out of his hand and bent it over her raised knee. The stick shattered into several pieces. She held the fresh break toward the deputy as she raised the old break.

He looked at the large splinters of the break from her knee. Some of the sharp shards were a couple of inches long and only tenuously attached. As he watched, two of the splinters fell from the stick. He pointed at the original break. "That's cleaner. Maybe not so violent."

Nash smiled. "Like the astronaut never crashed through the ceiling?"

His lower lip rolled as he thought. Slowly, he turned to look at the pile of debris. "There aren't any roof tiles."

Nash dipped her head. "That's a start." She leaned over and pulled out four sticks close to the same length. Holding them stacked four high, she leaned them on the floor and the tabletop, about eight inches higher. Watching the deputy, she stomped on the four sticks—breaking them. She held out the original broken stick and the original break. Fanning the four sticks, she held the fresh break next to the original.

Zap nodded. "Close. How do you figure?"

Nash rocked her head. "We have an Apollo astronaut who crashed through a roof and landed on a poker table and chairs in a saloon in the eighteen-nineties. Sound about right?"

"I guess. I never really thought about it like that. But yeah."

Nash surveyed the room with a critical eye. It was smaller than some of the dance halls she had seen, on or off bases. The ten tables were reminiscent of the office room Muna rearranged to create large tables. No matter how many desks she added, there was always room for more. This wasn't an uncrowded room but a spacious area designed for the functionality of space.

She pulled out her phone and checked the bars. She smiled at the four bars. *Another confirmation.* She found the number and pushed the green icon as she turned to study the deputy. "And you don't know how old this town is...?"

He shook his head.

"Hold on..." Nash could hear several people talking at once in the background. Ming came back to the phone. "Sorry. A lot is going on here right now. Thank you for calling Deep Six. This is Ming."

Nash burped a single chuckle. "It must be something crazy for you to answer your phone and not check the caller ID."

"Oh... Nash, we're trying to watch her shoot."

"Shoot what?"

The young woman almost screamed in exasperation. "Muna. She's shooting next, but the asshats went to a commercial break. If they don't show her shoot, I'm going to harvest some balls... well... send Jazz to do it. What's up?"

Nash looked around the room until she found Powder curled up in the large archway to the saloon. She looked like she was sleeping, but Nash doubted she had her eyes closed all the way. Not a reservation dog in a strange place.

"Can you ping my phone and see where I am?"

"Just a minute."

Nash could hear the soft clicking of the keyboard. She always wondered how the young kids could cradle their phones between their ears and shoulders. When she tried, she always hung up.

"You're in New Mexico, just east of... hmm... this is a joke, right? It's something shitty."

Nash peeked at the deputy. "It's Naschitti. Like NASCAR and cheating. What does it say is here?"

"Just a minute." The phone rustled from being held somewhere against the fabric. "Hey, Bunny? Nash needs to know where she is. No. Yes, now. That's why we're recording from six locations." The phone changed. "Nash, I'm shoving you over to Bunny. She wanted to know if you got blown up again. Great talking to ya. I'll text you the shooting score."

The older voice flowed through the phone. "Hey, Nash. I've got you in a low canyon three and a half miles west of Nas... are they kidding me?"

Nash chuckled. "Cheating. Like cheat misspelled. It's an Indian name. What do you see?"

"It looks like nineteen buildings lining the two sides of a single wide street. It looks like two streets running along the backs of the rows of buildings. You parked your... What are you doing in a regular car instead of an SUV? But you parked it at the east end of town."

Nash groaned as she held her hand over her face and the phone and lowered her voice. "Oh shit. Whose satellite did you tap into?"

The mother growled through gritted teeth. "I'm actively providing backup to a federal agent in the field. So stop asking pesky questions. What else do you need to know?"

"Yes, the white car's the only muscle car they had. No, it's not an SUV. And the locals think I'm standing in an old ghost town. I'm thinking not so much. I need to know everything I can about what's what and how long."

"Just a second. Um... nope. Nope. Nope. None there... and... nope. Nope. And none on the other side, either. You're on a movie set."

Nash frowned. "Excuse me?"

She could feel Bunny bending each finger back as she ran through her thinking. "Have you tried using a bathroom?"

"No." Nash frowned and turned toward the deputy. "Hey Zap, is there a bathroom in here? When you came here before, did any of you find a bathroom?"

He blinked. "I'll go look."

Nash watched the man stroll out to the saloon with purpose. "Powder. I need a bathroom. Help Zap find one." She pulled her phone back up to her ear. "What made you think of a bathroom?"

Bunny laughed. "Because I had a kid, and now I hit *the* age. Anywhere I go, the first thing I find is the bathroom. As for the town being an old ghost town, the answer's positively no. There isn't a single outhouse behind any of the buildings. And another thing, all the roofs look the same. Silver-gray tin. The aging or rust looks like the roofs all got done at the same time. And it's a movie set because they always bring their own portable potties. And even the super nose won't find you anything but the back wall of the building you're in. Get out now or hold it."

Nash looked at Powder sitting next to her. "Yeah, Powder says there's no inside potty. So now I need to go. If you could...?"

"I'm on it, boss. I'll find the building permits and owner's records, deeds, and any liens."

"Thanks. I think we're done here. I need to go find what Naschitti has in the way of a bathroom."

Bunny snorted. "I hope it's a clean one."

16

THE HOUSE

1959

THE YOUNG BLONDE stood in the cottage's large front window.
She marveled at the twenty-five divided-lite, almost floor-to-ceiling
wall of glass. She imagined sitting in the easy chair and watching
Hollywood Way with all the exciting people coming and going at
the studios. A small cat would be a pleasant companion in one's
lap. Something to provide a bit of warmth on a winter's night.

She adjusted the small flower vase on the doily as the car pulled
to the curb. She secreted the fallen petal in her hand as she opened
the front door. Celeste stopped by the bush at the door, dropped the
petal behind, and then walked along the walkway to the street and
the car.

The driver adjusted his hat as he opened the back door and
offered his hand. A woman took the hand as she swung her legs
and long dress out to the curb. "Thank you, Stuart. But if you could
please... pull?"

"Yes, miss."

Celeste watched quietly as she watched the struggle the woman had with her legs. She now understood why Mr. Magnuson had insisted on this house, with the master bedroom and bath on the main floor.

"Good afternoon, Miss Dorfman. Welcome to your new home. The moving crew arrived this morning, and I hope they've put everything away agreeably." She extended her hand. "I'm Celeste Dumont, your production assistant."

Betty squinted as she studied the young woman. "I don't think this relationship will work."

The young blonde choked back her smile. "I'm sorry...?"

Betty turned and pointed at the driver. "What's his name?"

Celeste's fall of pastel curls vibrated as she wrinkled her brow at the man. "Stuart?"

"And I'm to call you... by what name?"

"Celeste... or Miss Dumont, if you prefer?"

Betty slumped on her right hip as she pointed and talked. "So we have Stuart and Celeste, and the dog is Charlie, but we stick me with Miss Dorfman or, god forbid, ma'am."

"I'm..."

Betty winked back at Stuart. "You were right. She flusters easily."

The man laughed. "I said nothing of the kind. But you're right. She does."

Betty turned on Celeste. "All my life, I've heard Betty or Miss Dorfman. A few people have mistaken my polio legs for old age and called me Mrs. Dorfman." She rolled her eyes in exasperation. "I don't look a thing like my mother. I took after my father, and if I ever forget to pluck, my mustache will also be a large walrus projection. So, if I'm to start a new life in this house, with a career at the studios, let's take a gamble and choose. I favor the short and jauntiness of Bet. What do you two think?"

The young woman blinked at the taller man. "I feel like I just grabbed hold of a tornado and don't know how to let go."

He held up his palms with raised eyebrows. "Thankfully, I'm only the driver."

Betty barked a laugh. "But if I get the contract right, you're my driver. Bet or Betty?"

"All I'm going to say is that I'd never bet against you."

Betty turned back to the young woman. "Well, there we have it. Bet for the win. Now, about this house?"

—————

BET CLUTCHED HER NOTEPAD TO HER CHEST AS SHE entered the large office. She paused at the door. Looking about, she wasn't sure if she had entered Mister Magnuson's office or one of the grand oversized movie sets.

"May I help you?"

Bet started. "Oh. Oh... I wasn't expecting..." She waved her hand about the room. "All of this..." She spied the lamp and couch near the window and took a hesitant step. "Isn't this the couch in...?"

The secretary rose and walked around her desk with a smile. "You must be Betty Dorfman. Reggie mentioned you'd be in one day soon. I'm Sylvia, his personal secretary."

Bet turned and shook the hand as she evaluated the woman. "Five foot four. Wavey brown hair, perfect teeth, and a pleasant face." Bet smiled, "Straight out of Central Casting. And I go by Bet."

The woman rolled her eyes and shrugged. "Nothing so glamorous. I was working in the commissary. But I remembered Reggie liked the little prune Danishes they only had in the morning. So when I saw him, I snuck one out of the kitchen and set it on his plate. A few months later, he had sent me off to Mrs. Crumpstein's secretarial school in Pasadena. Would you like some coffee, tea, or lemonade, Bet? Reggie is down the lot, but I expect him back shortly."

"We started early this morning, so coffee would be grand, please. With only a little cream."

The woman turned to what looked like the one wall. Other than the handle, the folding door didn't show. The two small refrigerators under the counter cooled everything else a visitor might want.

Bet smirked impishly. "What if I wanted something stronger?"

Sylvia mirrored the devilish smirk and folded back the other side door. "If you don't see what you like, tell me. I'll have it stocked by the next time you visit." The mirrored bar shone with dazzling top-shelf liquor, enticing guests to indulge in its tempting offerings.

Bet blinked as she took in the world of the powerful. "I'll have to study what I'd like to try next."

"Next?" Sylvia handed her the cup and saucer.

Bet blushed. "Oh yes. I tried the champagne at the Christmas party last year. It almost made my legs not work. Then Reggie told me about all this, and my legs really became untrustworthy. I've been here almost two months, and I'm still waiting to wake up."

Sylvia closed the doors. "Let's sit over by the window. My window is the only one which looks out on the lot. Even Reggie doesn't have as grand a view, which might explain why he goes down all the time. So tell me, what does he have you doing?"

Setting her coffee on the small table, Bet adjusted her legs and sat. Her hand ran over the fabric of the couch. "I loved the pattern in the…um…"

Sylvia smiled. "Cat on a Hot Tin Roof. Yes, we got a special release for his basement theater. It was very hush-hush about who he entertained. Did you like it?"

Bet scowled playfully. "Did you know there was not a single cat in the movie? Why they named it such a thing, I'll never know. But it was quite the drama."

Sylvia opened her mouth and then closed it. "How often do you take in movies?"

Bet looked fondly at the couch. "This was my first one." Her head snapped around. "But we plan to see more. Reggie said he'd get some animal movies, but they were sad. But I don't want to see sad movies. I want happy ones. Don't you think?"

Sylvia mewed a small smile. "Maybe we need to spend some evenings down in Hollywood and take in different movies."

"Just two women… alone?"

"The best kind of dating. We get to choose where to eat, what movie, and what chocolate treat we want with our popcorn without a man's opinion. So it's a date. How about Friday evening?"

Bet leaned over with a stage whisper. "It sounds wicked and adventurous. Count me in."

"So…" Sylvia nodded at the notebook.

"Oh. Some notes about what I think might be problems and how we can solve them. I'm only trying to figure out where I can fit in."

"Where are you?"

Bet sipped and then put down her cup on the saucer. "Last month I started in wardrobe. Nothing made sense to me. I don't know or understand clothing. But this month, they moved me over to… props. Things like couches, tables, coffee cups, glasses, and even beds."

Sylvia nodded. "Set properties. We call them props for short."

Bet firmly smiled as she rocked her head and upper body. "Turns out I know little about furniture as well…" She rolled her eyes.

Sylvia cocked her head as she smiled shyly. "But…"

"It turns out I know more about guns than I thought. Pistols are pistols, but rifles, I know. They produced the animals we stuffed. And today, we checked back in seven of the eight cannons a crew had checked out. Who loses a cannon? They weigh a ton, and what are you going to do with them? Shoot cars from your front yard?"

"What did they say?"

Bet raised her arms in an imitation of the truck driver. "Lady, I drive the truck." She leaned forward. "Turns out, those cannons cost us four thousand dollars to make. Make. Who makes cannons these days? I'm talking about the kind in the Civil War. Wooden wagon wheels. The stick thing to shove the cannonballs down then..."

Laughing, Sylvia held up her palms. "Stop. My sides hurt. And so you know, many people make swords, as well as knives, for us. Even the chariots they used for Ben Hur. Everything gets made for movies. And you aren't the first to notice they don't always come back from the set locations. But you have an idea to stop it?"

Bet nodded. "Tracking numbers. On everything. Last month, we checked out two hundred eighty Civil War uniforms—one hundred sixty Union and one twenty South. Four didn't make it back, and seven were so badly damaged we had to throw them away. I calmly remarked to the production assistant that we would charge them two thousand for each uniform over and above the rental fees. Three of the uniforms showed up the next day."

Sylvia opened her mouth in mock horror. "You didn't."

Bet blushed. "I did. And got scolded for overstepping my place. The next day, the prop master's runner slipped me a brand new twenty with a wink. But even if they charge the production company for the damaged and lost uniform, they are still short those eight uniforms. What if someone needs everything they have, and they're short those eight?"

Sylvia leaned back against her chair. "You'll learn. We make more or have them made. But it doesn't justify not getting things returned."

"Who's not returning what?"

They turned and stood at the sound of the man's booming voice at the door.

Sylvia smiled. "Ah, the prodigal son returns. Just in time, Reggie. You can head the lynching party."

He smiled. "Hello, Betty. Good to see you found my lair and the bear I keep here. Who are we lynching?"

Sylvia interceded. "The production crews. Bet encountered the dirty little secret of the sticky fingers of stars and crew alike."

Reggie pointed at the notepad. Glancing at his office, he sat instead. "And you had some ideas about managing the inventory?"

Sylvia patted him on the shoulder. "I'll get you some coffee. You're going to want some."

17
BLAST OFF

Nash stared wide-eyed at the sheaf of paperwork. Her right hand fumbled on the desk for her mug or hydroflask of coffee.

The black flask with the FBI badge engraved on the side floated in the air next to the report. "More jet fuel, Miss?"

Nash blinked and looked at her flask and then to the face of the deputy director's right hand.

"Jeez, Donna, where did I leave it this time?"

"Well, not as bad as the ladies' room, but close. Near the empty burning coffee pot. The lid was off but with cold coffee. I made you fresh. I took a shot at three pink and a decent jolt of white paint. You sleeping okay? You've been off your norm for a few days now."

"Yeah… no. It's the couch. Mina needs her sleep, and the sandbox calls me back during the night. So the couch and Powder patrols all night long. Which part of me keeps track of—also all night."

The redhead leaned her thigh against the desk. "I would tell you a vacation is in order, but I don't think that would solve your nights. Are you talking to anyone?"

Nash's smirk was wan. "Do you count?"

"Only until the scotch takes effect. But seriously, it's not a weakness. And talking through things can help."

Nash tossed the report on her report-strewn desk as she sipped on her tall black flask. "I've been talking to Mina more. That helps. She understands now when I grab the extra blanket and my pillow. I just wish Powder would stay with her."

Donna winced. "I swore I'd never use my father's clichés... but a soldier does what a soldier does."

"Ouch."

"Too close to home?"

Nash swirled the coffee in her flask. "More than you know. Probably for all three of us. Well, now we have the nurse... so four. It's a low testosterone zone, but high-octane."

"What kind of nurse? If I can ask?"

Nash smiled as she pulled out her phone. "One that can cook in any restaurant she wants."

As Nash's phone chimed, Donna turned back to her desk. Nash picked up the phone and pushed the green icon. "I want it short and sweet. How soon do I leave?"

Muna giggled. "Tonight or tomorrow, your choice. Cape Kennedy or Johnson Space Center."

"What's behind tomorrow's door?"

"Johnson Space Center. Time to identify the suit."

Nash looked at Donna, trying not to seem obvious about eavesdropping. She remembered something Uncle had taught her. "Atsá bił naat'áanii bitsiiyéél, t'áá ádí yikáá' gidísh."

The silence at the other end struck Nash as funny as watching Donna throw up her hands and turn her chair around to face the wall.

"Muna?"

Pure Muna, her gut growl vibrated the phone. "You mispronounced coyote, but I liked the nitty Yiddish goldfish. Now I don't know who's hanging out with Uncle too much. But I assume you're at work with Miss Nosey Listening."

"Yah-ta-hey."

"Did you get me a trinket or at least a matchbook?"

"Nothing there but a gas station. I got gas, but even the receipt says Chevron station four seventy-six. What's in Texas?"

"NASA space people. They are bigger geeks than me. They want to see the helmet and the gloves."

"Why me? It sounds like a geek run."

Muna mumbled something. "Sorry, I had to tell Chips and Baby something. What were you saying?"

"Why…" Nash held her phone out—circled her thumb and ring finger in her mouth—and whistled with her shrillest Marine catcall. Returning the phone to her ear. "You heard me the first time."

Muna's voice was dialed back to the junior agent. "Because I got a phone call."

Nash hummed the Jeopardy theme song and glanced over to see Donna glaring from her desk and the deputy director standing in his doorway. She ignored the other agents standing to see what the whistle was about. "I have an audience."

"It was your wife."

Nash hummed, "Gotta go." Pushing the disconnect, she stood and stretched to look at the rest of the agents diving for their desks.

Walking to the deputy director, she stopped and held her right hand toward Donna. The paperwork crunched against her thumb. Nash held it out to the deputy director.

Tony didn't look. "Where're you going?"

"Houston for a few days."

"Is that enough time?"

Nash lowered one eyelid. "If not, I'll come back via a couple of weeks in Barbados."

"Bring me back a couple of bottles."

"Go earn your own."

He chuckled. "Come catch me up."

He dropped the paperwork on his clean desk and sank into his chair.

Donna slid in and slapped Nash's black flask into Nash's hand. "You left it on your desk again. But you mispronounced gang." She winked and turned, closing the door quietly.

The deputy director frowned. "Gang?"

Nash rolled her eyes. "The Navajo saying goes something like *when the coyote calls his gang, time to run.*" She leaned forward. "Did I tell you she's scary?"

"I already know. And she knew what you said?"

Nash ballooned her furled lips and grew her eyes as she shrugged.

Tony pointed at the paperwork.

"We're going down to Johnson Space Center to talk to NASA. They want to see the helmet and the gloves."

Tony frowned. "For what?"

Nash took a sip from her flask and realized Donna had refilled it with fresh, hot coffee. "If I knew the answer, I'd be a rocket scientist. But my squint says come. Something about being lead and therefore the top of the Incident Command Structure."

"Who else is involved?"

"NASA."

He vibrated his head behind the coffee mug. "No. That's Muna's wheelhouse. Who else participates in making you the top of the ICS?"

"My wife."

He stared at his agent for more than a few heartbeats and one blink. Leaning forward, he clicked his pen and scrawled his name on the paperwork.

"Taking the dog?"

"I'll talk to the boss."

THE AIR FORCE STAFF SERGEANT DROVE THE YUKON. Muna and Nash optioned the backseat. Muna pointed at the large center console. Nash nodded. "She preferred the cushy mommy bed instead of another boring day at work." Nash glanced over at the hard, tight bun. "How long did Andy say the bun's good for?"

The half-drooped eyes glinted a steaming glace at the senior agent. "Until I get over only coming in second."

Nash knew the sentiment. "So you wash, and he pulls the croquet ball. It must be a bitch to sleep on."

"I'm a side sleeper. Can we drop it?"

Nash gazed out the side window and spoke to the glass. "Sure, whiner. So, no Paris?"

"Alternate."

As they passed through the checkpoint, Muna mussed. "I expected more static displays of rockets or spaceships…"

The sergeant peered through the rearview mirror at her. "You're thinking of the tourist trap in Florida. This is a working space center. But they don't launch from here. This is control. We do the work so the kids can go play with the toys."

Muna chuckled. "Nah. We've been to Disney World. They have all the kiddie rides."

A woman in a white lab coat stood waiting in the building's doorway. The sergeant pulled to a stop but didn't open the doors. His job was transport. Drive only. His hands were to be on the wheel with the engine running—at all times. Muna frowned, but Nash pushed her out. "Thanks, sergeant. We'll call when we need the ride back out."

He nodded and watched in the rearview mirror as Nash retrieved the bulky satchels from the back. The SUV rolled away at the click of the back doors.

"Oh, good. We feared you might have brought photos." She held out her hand. "Major Grimm. Guthrie or Gert. My father was a huge folk music fan."

Nash thought about the woman's age and gave up. "Arlo or Woody?"

The woman chuckled. "My oldest brother's Woody, and then

came Arlo. When I showed up, only one name was left, and my mother refused to have another Mary in the house. So I got Guthrie. Let's see what you found."

The lab reminded Muna of San Francisco, but the autopsy tables were more chemistry worktables. She stood in the middle and slowly turned around, taking it all in.

"And you're looking for…?"

Muna stopped and looked back at Nash and Gert. "Wondering where you're hiding an old guy who looks like Einstein and his Tinman partner."

Nash leaned toward the major. "Ignore her. She thinks she's back in the autopsy lab in San Francisco."

Gert shrugged her shoulders and face. "Nothing so macabre. The autopsies we perform here are on equipment failures."

Nash set the large satchel on the table and unzipped it. "Well, as requested, we have helmets and gloves, and we threw in the boots just in case."

She lifted the gloves and placed them on the table. The boots were next, followed by the helmet.

Bringing over a laptop, the major booted it to an application. The cursor blinked in a box marked *Item Number*.

Picking up the first glove, she rolled back the gaiter to expose the aluminum ring. Turning it, she found the two lines of numbers. Squinting, she read the letters and numbers. She grumbled a throat clearing as she entered the digits into the box and hit return. The box shook and cleared.

She glared at Nash and picked up the second glove. Same results.

Rolling down the gaiters on the boots, she tried both sets of numbers and both lines. Still a shake and a clearing.

Rolling over the helmet, she found the codes. She picked up the right glove and looked at the codes again. "These aren't ours."

"But…?"

She held up a finger. "Give me a minute." Turning, she left the laboratory.

Muna leaned against the stainless-steel table. "What do you think?"

Nash yawned and looked around. "I think I hate dead-ends as much as I dislike wild-goose chases."

"Especially when your goose gets roasted. But if it's not theirs, whose?"

Nash shrugged as she looked closely at the numbers on the glove's ring. "How much did Mike and Oz find on our body?"

"The zombie? Nothing. There weren't any fingerprints left to pull. Even if the tanning didn't remove them, the years and use had worn down the ends enough to remove any ridges. So all we have is the eight ball tattoo. I'll let you guess at how many hits I got on that search."

Nash snorted a single grump. "Between bikers, junkies, pool hustlers, Navy, and Marines, their multiple spouses, children, and bowlers... more than a few. Your computer is probably still counting."

"Accurate guess."

"I brought all three rings to try." The major returned with a ring around her neck and two on her wrists. "I feel like I should be featured in a National Geographic article. Except I'm not taking my clothes off."

"Good choice. What are the rings?"

Gert handed one to Nash and one to Muna. "These are check rings. We can match them to the rings on the suits to check the lock and seal." She rolled the helmet over and removed the ring from her neck. Placing it in the neck ring on the helmet, she rotated the locking mechanism. Everything seated. The six dogs engaged, and the final lock pushed in. It was a perfect match. She nudged her chin at Muna to try the glove. The final lock pushed in with a small click.

They watched Nash slide her ring into the boot's ring. The

keeper ring closed as she rotated the ring. Pushing on the final seating slide, she was rewarded with a soft click.

The major examined each. "There's only one other test. I'll be right back. Wait, better yet, bring the glove and boot."

They walked deeper into the building. The major held the helmet cocked in her arm like she had flown with it. Muna finally slipped the glove over her right hand.

Nash glared at her. "If you try to moonwalk with the glove, I'm going to kick your Michael Jackson ass into next week with this boot."

Gert turned and walked backward. "Buzz, during his last landing, tried to moonwalk. It got some laughs, but toys aren't supposed to bend like that." Her mouth pressed into a mew so as not to smile at her joke.

Nash rolled her eyes. "I hope you didn't tell that joke to Buzz Aldrin."

Gert stopped and pointed at a door. "Here we are. And it was Neil who told the joke at Buzz's retirement party." She pushed open the door. "Pressure lab two-oh-one. We're over here."

She led the way to a table next to two large hoses hanging out of the wall. Gert paused, unlocked the ring on the helmet, and slid the catch to release the ring. She pointed out how the rings worked.

"These small, tapered rods, called dogs, pull back when you open the ring. This releases the joined ring. If you're putting them on, you can just push them together. If all six dogs spring back into place, the ring can turn, and the final lock will engage." She turned the ring and pointed at the small triangle arrow moving from the single line to the triple line. The ring seated, and she pushed in the final lock-in. "If one dog doesn't seat, you can't turn this ring, and the final won't push in. In space, this last check on every connection is important."

She grabbed the largest hose hanging from the wall. Nash and Muna recognized the now familiar ring. Gert pushed it into place until she heard the pins click. Turning the ring, she pushed the final lock. She pointed at one of the other hoses. "I think number seven will be your glove. And the boot is... number one."

The agents removed the text rings and hooked the glove and boot to the wall hoses. Gert pushed the buttons over the three suit parts and then flipped the switches on the main control panel. The hoses inflated.

Muna poked at the inflated hose connected to her glove. It dimpled. "How much pressure?"

The scientist in the major smiled. "How much do you know about boiling water at high altitudes?"

Muna smiled. "I know we can't make hot coffee on the fourth floor."

The woman frowned. "Why is that?"

Nash laughed. "Because the coffee pot is on the third floor."

"Does the FBI ever get serious about their work?"

Nash sobered. "Too often. It's the major autopsy and forensic lab for the Pacific Northwest. But they get stuff like this from New Mexico or a couple of freezers filled with dead bodies from the California desert."

Muna watched as the woman's face blanched. "Then there were the twenty-two bodies found at the commune on the Arizona border. Or the twenty-seven skeletons dredged from a place called Bone Creek..."

The woman held up her palms. "Okay. I'm sorry. We're just a lot more serious around here."

"But your question about boiling water?"

"Actually, that is just the start. So at sea level, water boils at 212°F. But the temperature drops a degree or two for each one thousand feet of elevation as the pressure reduces. On Mount Everest, the pressure is lower, and your coffee boils at only one sixty. Warm, but not so satisfying. But at the International Space Station, your blood can boil at ninety-eight degrees. So the space station and the suits are only pressurized to about a pound or two above where your blood will boil."

Nash tapped on the helmet. "Why not pressurize to a safer margin of error, like five or ten pounds?"

The major smirked as she turned to the control panel. She thumbed a roller wheel as she watched a small readout. The helmet moved, but the hoses on the other two straightened until the hose and glove stuck straight out. The boot was only a slight droop.

"That's five pounds over the boiling point. Poke the hose now?"

Muna poked at the hose. And then, using both hands, tried to squeeze the hose.

"Now, in space, for every action, there's an equal and opposite reaction. Or with a rock-stiff suit, there's no ability to move."

She pointed at the larger readouts on the monitors over each hose. All read zero-point-zero.

"These check for leaks. As you can imagine, a leak, even a tiny pinhole, can propel you away from the space station. So we check the suits and connections constantly."

She turned off the pressure wall, and the hoses collapsed.

Muna unhooked the glove. "So, now what?"

The woman's eyes were pinned wide as she slowly wagged her head. "I'm baffled. They look like ours. They connect perfectly with ours, but... the numbers don't match. So we call the big gun in New York."

18

TOUCH DOWN

THE MAN still sat at the desk, covered with models of rockets and a lunar lander. A space shuttle and some other spaceships from TV hung suspended in the air overhead. The shelves behind him seemed even more jammed with photos and other memorabilia.

He wiggled the thin white mustache. "Good afternoon, Huston. Do we have a problem?" He chuckled. "I always wanted to say that. What's up, Gert?"

The major pointed at the computer screen and then the agents. "Dick Sharp, NASA knowledge repository extraordinaire, I'd like you to meet FBI Agents Muna al-Faragi and Nash Running Bear."

He smiled. "How did you do in Colorado, Muna?"

Muna's eyes crushed to half squint as she growled. "Second."

"Ouch. But you're on the team?"

"Alternate."

"Hmm… double ouch. So what do we have now?"

"If someone on the team…"

He laughed and waved his hand in the air. "No. The astronaut suit."

"Oh, here's Gert." Muna rolled her eyes with a smile.

The major eased into the center. "It's the rings, Dick. They

119

brought down the helmet, gloves, and boots. The rings match perfectly. The units look authentic to me. Well, the helmet's missing the inner pressure globe and com units. But they appear to be NASA."

"So what's the problem, Gert?"

She glanced at Nash. "The numbers are wrong."

He leaned back and crossed his arms. "Try me."

She held up the glove. "Gama Alpha Sierra one niner seven six…"

He held up his hand. "Hold on. Gama Alpha would fit the early Apollo, but Sierra? Are you sure it's not a nine?"

The major handed it to Muna. "Sierra, sir. Then there's a dash before the numbers."

"Okay. Gama Alpha Sierra. Now give me the numbers again."

Muna offered the glove back, but the major pointed at the computer monitor.

Dick Sharp looked up from his notepad. "Is there a problem?"

Muna gave the major side-eye. "No, sir. Just working out the logistics. Your numbers are one, niner, seven, six, five, niner."

His face wrinkled.

The major growled. "What's wrong?"

He glanced up. "Are there any numbers after a dash or something?"

Muna shook her head. "Not on the first line. Just the three letters and six numbers."

"Okay, give me the suit number."

Muna frowned and looked at the major. "The what number?"

The man looked up from two thousand miles away. "Sorry. It's the second line. The first line is the mission and suit style. The second is the suit identification number. Allen Shepherd's suit starts with Alpha Sierra. Buzz, Beta Alpha, and so forth."

Muna nodded. "Got it." She held up the glove ring. "Oscar Sierra November dash zero two three dash three." She looked up.

The man looked at a wall they couldn't see. "It's fourteen forty-seven your time. I'll call you back at sixteen hundred. I need to hash this out. Did the other numbers match up to these?"

Gert's shoulders slumped. "I'll text you all the numbers on your cell phone."

He half stood. "Perfect. I'll get on these rogue designators and get back to you." His screen blanked.

Muna looked at Nash. "Coffee?"

Nash looked at the major. "Anything here worth consuming?"

The woman chuckled as she gently shook her head. "I grew up within spitting distance of the Okefenokee Swamp. You're describing everything other than gator toenails and teeth."

Nash held out her thumb and little finger in a fist and moved it back and forth between them. "Same. Anything a step above roadkill?"

The major glanced at her watch. "If Suzie's still cooking, we can get a turkey melt and some fries. But I'll still vote for the coffee."

"THE TWENTY-FIVE METERS IS THE CLOSEST TO WHAT I regularly shoot, except it's only a twenty-two long rifle bullet. There's no high-pressure loading or choice of wadcutter or nose, but it's supersonic straight from the box. And everything's off-the-shelf ammo."

The major straddled the stool and leaned her elbows on the stainless-steel table. "But the air pellet is…?"

"Four-point-five millimeter or .177 caliber." Muna held up her hand with the thumb and finger held close together. "Slightly thinner than the twenty-two, but half the length. You don't see any deflection, but the hit power is reduced. And in my hand, there isn't any kick."

"So, the air gun at the ten, but the live round for the twenty-five."

Muna's eyes drifted shut as she rocked her nod. "And as sexist as it sounds, only the guys shot the fifty-meter."

"With the twenty-two long rifle."

Muna squinted one eye and cocked her head for the yes. "So I don't really care about being sexed out. If we're going to shoot only half a football field, let's make it fun with at least nine millimeters."

Nash snorted. "Or open it up to the fifty calibers."

The major grimaced. "Barretts?"

Muna waved her hand in disgust. "Nah, those are milers. She's talking about my Desert Eagle and my Smith & Wesson five hundred. They're both fifty calibers."

The woman stared at Muna's hands.

Nash barked a short laugh. "Don't let size confuse you. Those hands beat on a keyboard all day long after a grueling morning routine of hundreds of rounds through each of her seven guns. Don't arm wrestle her. She'll crush your hand before you start."

The computer dinged. The major looked at the clock. "Right on time." She hit the keyboard, and the screen lit up. "Right on time, Sharpie."

"Well, sort of. I still didn't find two of the numbers. But I have my suspicions where they came from."

"So what is definite?"

He looked at Nash. "Well, Agent Running Bear, it's a hike for you, but down the state from Agent al-Faragi. Your source is in the greater Los Angeles area."

Muna raised her hand. "I'll take Jet Propulsion Laboratories for a thousand, Alex."

He smiled as he pointed his finger, then shook his head. "Close by twenty miles. But halfway between the ivory tower on the mountain and Lockheed Marten. Sylmar, to be exact. Your inquiry is going to be a company called Orbital Surplus. Hence your Oscar Sierra designation."

"But if they're just a military surplus seller, where did they get them?"

He smirked. "They made them. Well, their parent company, Global Effects Lab, did. Over time, NASA carelessly discarded or lost scores of artifacts, never giving a thought to establishing museum exhibits, especially across different states, such as Long Island, Florida, Oklahoma, and Texas. As a result, they needed to reconstruct them, but cheaper than the originals. Luckily, the skilled individuals at Global Effects Lab had decades of experience in creating props for films. By giving them precise blueprints, we enhanced their already impressive craftsmanship, including the machined connectors that brought you into our world. I suspect the reason their replicas flawlessly matched ours is thanks to those blueprints."

Muna held up the glove. "Who made these originally?"

He shrugged. "Any number of contractors were involved in everything from the screws to toilet seats. North American Aviation, Grumman Corp., Rocketdyne, Douglas Aircraft, and even General Motors, to name the big ones. Then, there are smaller ones like Ford, IBM, Carrier, and FMC, but each of those contractors didn't make all their parts in-house, so you have a thousand little guys. In the Seattle area, they had a saying. When Boeing sneezed, the entire area caught a cold. Hundreds of little shops, one to five-person machine shops, made one or two parts for Boeing. So part numbers are important. Something to allow us to know the original contractor and who they farmed the work out to."

She looked at the part number on the glove's locking ring. "And this Orbital Surplus...?"

"It's the same guy..." He rose on his hip and fished for his wallet. "Wait, a minute..." The wallet reminded Muna of her father's. Maybe he needs a single credit card and driver's license, but a bulging wallet full of business cards he might use one day.

"Here it is. Chris Gilman. Nice guy. I worked with him on the lunar landing set for the museum down in Oklahoma. If you show an interest in what he's holding, he'll give you a college class on its origin, purpose, and why it is no longer in use." Pulling out his phone, he took a close-up of the card. "I just texted it to you, Gert. You can share with them."

Muna glanced over at Nash. "Los Angeles…"

"I'm thinking… on it. Powder is a minor…" Her thumbs typed on her phone. As she rested it on the table, it vibrated in response.

She turned it over and smiled. She thumbed the green icon. "Good afternoon, James. How's my favorite air magician?"

"On top of the world, Nash. Well, laying here on the sofa with a bulldog on each hip. Miss Daisy is having a play date. What's the problem?"

"Powder is a minor."

The man's laugh was juicy as it was full of gut. "Hardly. She's more of a major, but what's the problem?"

"I'm in Houston, and I need to go to Los Angeles."

"Magic Rick can manage that…"

"Powder is in D.C. with her other mommy."

"Oh."

Nash could hear his phone scratching on his beard.

"We're more used to spoiled, two-legged eight-year-olds going to visit the grands…"

"So the nurse would have to accompany the dog…"

Nash could picture the clinking on the phone as the man removing his heavy Clark Kents and massaging the bridge of his nose. Something she watched him do as he studied a problem further back on the plane. As a senior flight attendant, he usually performed the duties of the purser and all-around problem fixer.

"Let me make a call. I'll call you back in a couple of minutes. Which airport in Los Angeles?"

Nash looked at the man on the screen. "Where would we need to land, Dick?" She ignored the lecherous comment on her phone.

"Burbank. It's a thirty-minute drive from the airport."

"Thanks." She brought up her phone. "Did you hear that, you nasty-minded young man?"

James laughed. "Still older than you. Yes, Burbank—Been Under

Remodel—for years. I'll call you right back." The phone snicked closed.

Muna raised an eyebrow. "Do we call Magic Rick before or after our favorite queen waves her wand?"

The major contorted her face. "Magic Rick, queens, wand?"

Nash snorted. "Magic Rick is our travel guru. Both he and James are our favorite funcles—fun uncles. They're gay and lean heavily into the queen land at the least provocation. But they are both amazing at their jobs."

"And James does...?"

"A flight attendant with thirty-five years of seniority. And... we've kind of adopted him into our family... or we into his. Either way, it all works."

"And the problem now?"

Muna rocked with a soft snort. "We're here. We need to go to Burbank." She pointed at Nash. "But her K-9 is in D.C. and needs to be working."

Nash bobbled her head. "Not really. There's no clear and present need... but technically..."

"So where's the dog?"

Her phone vibrated. "In bed with her other mommy." She thumbed the icon. "Yeah, James."

"I'll collect my niece at seven tonight. Lele will have her ready. We'll non-revenue to Burbank on the red eye. Rick can text me your flight times, and we'll meet you in the morning. I'll go back to work out of LAX on Thursday, so I have a couple of days, and you know I need to be entertained."

"I don't know how entertaining we'll be. We're going to go talk NASA parts with someone who makes them for movies or something."

The drama queen slipped into his deep territory. "Oh yes. That boring flight stuff. Here, let me go dust off my Saturn rocket model, the Space Shuttle model with the working arm, and my eighth-scale model of Friendship 7."

Nash laughed. "Okay, you're in. But don't wear your uniform and try to wiggle a flight attendant job on the next shuttle."

"Oh gawd. Shuttle? Girl, we haven't flown those since last century."

Nash growled into the phone. "Goodnight, James. And don't spoil my daughter."

"Hah."

19

TAKING FLIGHT

EVERY AIRPORT SMELLED SIMILAR. Inside the buildings, they seemed to all use the same cleaners, same carpets, same wall paint, and smell the same—many sweaty bodies in confined spaces. But the swoosh of the sliding glass doors to the outside brought the true, unique smell of each location. Dulles smelled like rotting politics washed by the polluted waters of the Potomac River. In New Orleans, Nash always said the chronic humidity worsened the rotting vegetation of the back bayous. The sharp salt smell coming off the bay spiced San Francisco. But the aging former star for celebrities and movie stars to sneak into town had a smell rooted in desert-level heat, old motor oil, and extra money. Companies in the early 1900s spilled or buried toxic fuels and manufacturing waste near the neighborhoods of their workers. Old oil wells became capped, or pipes buried. The iconic grasshopper oil pumps became eyesores and legislated out of sight. Some still worked in large tin warehouses, and other wells were drained by pumps miles away. But the sins and stains stay from the heydays of World War II and then the push into space. And the unique smell hit Nash and Muna, exiting the terminal.

James stood wearing black slacks, a white dress shirt, and a chauffeur's hat, which looked more like a pilot's hat.

Pulling his dark glasses down his nose, he gawked at Muna, pushing a luggage cart. "Oh girl, you'll never make it as a flight attendant unless you learn how to pack a hell of a lot lighter than this." Strolling to the back doors of the black SUV. Lifting the large satchel, he shook his head. "Gurl, unless you planned to attend some AME church, you didn't need to pack an out-to-your-shoulders Sunday hat."

Muna gave him a cold side-eye as she handed him the other large satchel. "It matched the boots and gloves." There was no comment about the two small rucksacks James was used to seeing both agents pack. A weekend or a month, the rucks never changed.

Nash stood by the passenger door, looking at the dog statue through the window. Powder sat on the center console, watching straight ahead.

As James and Muna came around, Nash rolled her eyes toward James. "I take it she didn't like getting dragged away from her mommy and the spoiling food from Lele?"

"Everything was fine until she figured it out. We weren't just going for a short drive. I've suffered warmer frostbite. Even the other flight attendants at the dorm complained about the unseasonable cold front. But she's here, and it's all between you and her now."

Nash shifted her eyes to Muna, reaching for the back door. "Nope. You ride up front with your sister."

Muna shifted places. As she moved past James, she made her demands. "We need a cheap gas station for jerky."

James fluttered his lips in a raspberry as he airplaned his arms and turned to take command of the vehicle. "Check the glove box. Sorry, Nash. No scotch once we have touched down."

The neighborhood of tilt-up industrial buildings shared the streets with cracked stucco homes from the boom time of paychecks and postwar. Only occasionally rested an iconic stripped car on blocks in a front yard. The times had changed, and gentrification crept slowly into the pocket of the larger valley.

James stopped as the GPS ran out. The sign was almost a hello from the shy girl in the class. He backed up and then nosed the SUV into the small fenced-off parking lot in front. Only the small sports car hinted at anybody being there.

Muna grabbed the helmet satchel as the front door opened. The man filling the doorway smiled. "We're unarmed. No need for assault weapons. And we can lend you any swords, pikes, knives, or Ninja throwing stars if it comes to any kind of conflict."

Nash turned at James's soft sigh. "Oh, be still my beating heart. Please say this tall, curly, and handsome is who we're to see."

"Behave, James. Or I'll tie you up at the fire hydrant." She pulled the other satchel out of the back. "Doors, James."

Powder sniffed around at the knees and then turned and sat next to the man who had stopped at the search. "Did I just get searched for drugs, guns, or bombs?"

Nash chuckled. "Pet her head. If she leans into your leg, you were searched and found in possession of a beating heart. Otherwise, she was making sure you weren't today's body dump. Hi. Agent Nash Running Bear and that's Powder."

Muna stuck her hand out. "Agent Muna al-Faragi and our escort is James Prentice. Driver, flight attendant, and adopted uncle, brother, sister, or goofball."

The man bent and took the large satchels. "Chris Gilman. Welcome to Global Effects Laboratory." He raised the satchels to his six and a half feet in height. "And I'm assuming these are the items of interest. Come on in, and we'll grab a table."

The entry hall stretched out, lined with large, framed movie posters of the company's past work. Most they had seen and the others they had heard of. James pointed at the Predator poster. "Now here was one tall, dark, and handsome I didn't like."

Chris glanced back. "We won an Oscar for that."

Muna stood looking at the poster predating her birth. "For...?"

"We had been working on a suit, kind of like what you saw in Dune. Except it only covered the core body parts—the thighs and torso. We needed to keep camera operators who stood in warm swimming pools all day, warmer. It sounds silly, but a pool heated to eighty can kill someone standing in it up to their belly all day. Most only got pneumonia, but a few died of hypothermia. Because it's a warm pool and we're in Southern California, nobody thinks of hypothermia. But when the body core temp drops to ninety-five, your body starts shutting down. So we were working on a layer of tubes to keep the body core at the right temp."

Muna tapped the glass on the poster.

"And my good friend, Kevin Peter Hall, was complaining about how hot it got in the costume suits. We put temperature sensors in a gorilla suit, and within an hour, the temperatures were over one forty. So I made him a suit with the connectors at the back of the neck. So when they weren't shooting, we could raise a small flap and plug him in. The water would cool him down, but also the suit. With the sensors in various places in the suit, we could monitor his working conditions." He turned toward the end of the hall and his office. "We even built him a skullcap to chill his head. When your head is cool, you feel and think better."

"Oh yes. I love cool..."

Nash snapped her head around and glared at James. He put his finger and thumb to his lips and zipped them shut.

"Holy wars... Where did this come from?"

They stepped into the large office and looked at the deep blue and gold suit of armor standing in front of Muna. Nash and James sighed simultaneously.

Chris stood next to the suit. "This is my faithful reproduction of the last dress suit of adaptive armor built by the Royal Almain Armory in Greenwich, which was started by Henry the Eighth. This suit is referred to as the Greenwich Armor. As you can see, the extra pieces hanging on the wall make this suit adaptable to ground warfare, horse battle, or even jousting, just by adding or swapping out the pieces." He rested his hand on the suit. "This suit took me twenty years to make in my spare time. The original armory would have had dozens of masters, their fellow craft, and apprentices working on it for a few years."

Muna hovered her fingers at the gold lacework down the breastplate. "Is that actual gold?"

"Yes. However, where they would have applied gold by hammering it into the etching, we used electricity to perform the same function but with plating instead of fill. Faster, and less gold."

James swallowed. "How much does it weigh?"

Chris waved his hand in an all-encompassing sweep. "All of the armor put together weighs one twenty. But even in the heaviest configuration, which is for jousting, would be about eighty pounds." He pointed at Muna's and Nash's bodies. "You're wearing what, level two body armor?"

Nash held up her thumb and two fingers. "Three."

Muna groaned. "We've both been shot and blown up. You learn. But it's not plate."

"But it's heavy when you first pick it up. More than a gallon of milk. But once it's on, you get used to it."

Muna held up her two fingers. "Two gallons and it feels scary to be out of it."

"But not comfortable enough to sleep in it."

Muna coughed into her fist. "Speak for yourself."

Nash nodded with raised eyebrows. "I have a dog with me. But sometimes, it's like sleeping in your favorite pajamas. It was months before I finally gave up my thirty-pound battle plate when I got back from the sandbox. It's what you get used to. But it looks like this suit would be stiff to move around in."

Chris picked up a sleeve made of bands of metal connected by strips of fabric. "Here we are six hundred years later, but we learned from the old armor. These rings slide over each other to collapse on the inside of the elbow or knees, but the connecting strips of fabric allow for the arm to twist." Grabbing the extra arm off the wall, he pointed at the rivets. "The rivets hold these plates to a woven band. This rivet here is loose." He flexed the elbow. "So the plates slide over each other."

Muna smiled, took the arm, and moved it as she studied how it worked. "This only took Henry to France, but Neil went to the moon and back."

Chris rocked his head. "And all the same principles applied. Notice the rim here. The glove lays over this but isn't attached."

"So the knight can twist his wrist. Smart."

Chris flipped up the face shield on the helmet and opened the front like a couple of doors. He pointed at the rim of the neckpiece. "Here is the true genius. The helmet locks on this ring." He swung the doors shut and locked them. Grabbing both sides, he turned the head. "But they ride around on the guide. And the rivets to the cloth bands are still working here." He tipped the helmet side to side and back and forward. "As confining as a turtleneck sweater."

Nash moaned. "Speak for yourself."

James leaned into her shoulder. "It better be damn cold." They bumped the backs of their fists as the other two put the fancy armor back.

Chris nudged his chin out at the satchels. "Let's see what you brought. Dick Sharp is pretty sure this is some of our work."

Muna opened the helmet bag and lifted the helmet. "We might as well start with the big guy."

Chris flipped the helmet over and found the numbers on the ring. "Yup. It's ours. But let me look up this number. Are all the numbers matching?"

Nash vibrated her head. "No. The top numbers match. But..."

Chris's face soured. "Yeah, I had a props manager who, well, wasn't beyond obfuscating what things were where and what we were collecting. Let's start with this one." He strolled to his desk and sat, turning to the computer on the credenza.

He entered the numbers in his search box. The computer changed to a list of numbers and descriptions. "Ouch." He leaned forward and scanned down the list. Finally, he went back to the search box and typed in the word *helmet*. The screen refreshed and only showed seven entries. His mouth pulled to one side.

"You had the gloves and boots also?"

Muna turned and fished out one of each. She placed them on the desk. He grabbed the glove and typed in the numbers. One entry showed up.

He threw his hands in the air. "We have a winner." He clicked on the entry. The screen cleared, and another screen took its place.

"Four-month rental. Went out July twentieth, in nineteen. Location is Ghost Ranch, New Mexico. Never returned. Insurance paid the replacement on seven twenty-two." He swiveled around.

"Where did you find it?"

Nash smirked, pointing at the computer. "In a ghost town's saloon in New Mexico."

Muna growled. "There was a body in it."

Horror filled the man's face. "An actual body?"

Nash rolled her eyes. "Sort of."

Muna shivered. "The skin was."

James's face froze. "Tell me you're just saying that to give me nightmares."

Nash vibrated her head. "Tattoo and all."

"Just the skin..."

Muna pulled out her phone and scrolled through her photos. Turning the phone sideways, she held it out to Chris.

He pinched the screen and zoomed in. "It's a set dummy. Wow... do those lacings work?"

"Do they slide through the grommets when you sit it up? Yeah. At first, I thought it was laced like my shoes." She zigzagged her finger back and forth. "But as I really looked, the lacing is loose, and three different lacings overlap each other. So when you need a longer lace in the back, it pulls the extra lace from the stomach." She smiled and pointed back at the medieval armor.

Chris nodded. "Yes, but still ingenious. Most are just rag dolls and move the same. But Burbank Studios, back in the day, had some you could curl real-looking fingers around to hold a cocktail glass. They had an armature structure allowing them to pose the dummy, so they didn't need extras for a crowd scene."

Muna took her phone back and found the next photo. The dummy was sitting on the edge of the autopsy table. One leg crossed over the other, and it was smoking a stick of jerky.

"Exactly." He laughed at the pose. "It looks like a coroner's…"

Nash growled. "It is."

James held his hand over his eyes with the fingers slit. "I can't look. Well… maybe just a peek."

20
CHASING DUMMIES

CHRIS HUNG up the phone and swiveled around. "All the set dummies got sold to Universal. Many of Burbank's records are dead-ends, and they'll have created new records at Universal. But I'll reach out…" He glanced at his watch. "After lunch, and see who I can send you to."

Nash glanced at her watch. The morning's *five-minute tour* had taken over three hours—but felt like five minutes. And she wanted more. "Can we take you to lunch?"

He held up his watch and his right finger. An air horn tooted three times out in the driveway. "Sure. It's a hot truck, and Maria and her granddaughter make the best Mexican food the neighborhood offers."

Muna smirked. "And in this barrio, that's saying a lot."

Chris pointed at her. "Exact a Mundo, Chica."

Powder wasn't the only one licking her chops.

"I never thought pulled beef would beat reconstituted roadkill jerky, but wow. I need our nurse to spend a few days working the truck or just straight up kidnap Maria."

Chris chuckled as he dropped into his chair. "I think the neighborhood would hunt you down. I've seen the truck at a local church on Sundays, and I know if I mention working Saturday, she squeezes us in. But Monday through Friday, they are out there and set up at one o'clock sharp."

Muna sat on the couch with Powder between her and James. "Seven days a week?"

Chris rocked in his chair. "Self-employed, and hundreds depending on you every day."

James nodded soberly. "I know the feeling. I'm not flying the airplane, but..."

Nash sat studying Muna.

The smaller agent turned. "What?"

Nash snorted softly. "When was the last time you took a day off? Just for you. Left the building alone all day?"

James leaned forward and looked around Powder. "Left the building? Where do you work? From home?"

Her protest ran out of air, fast. "No... kind of..."

Nash noticed the frown creeping across Chris's face. "She's the tech nerd working the forensics lab in San Francisco. Labs are on the third floor, dorms are on the fourth, and there is a shooting range in the sub-basement. She's got nine restaurants on speed dial for delivery. Her go-to breakfast spot is three-quarters of a mile away. If you're feeling adventurous, Chow Fat's a mile walk through Golden Gate Park at night."

Muna leaned forward and buried her face in her hands. "Now you're making me sound pathetic."

James reached over and patted her head. "It's all good. You've had a hard few years. With getting shot up, blown up, and pistol-whipped to a broken jaw, and all. Now you need some funcle time with your uncle Jimmy. Now tell me about this dorm setup."

Chris widened his eyes at Nash. "I'm calling Universal. This is more drama than I get doing movies."

Nash stood. "I'm going to walk the little bladder."

Chris pointed at the workshop. "She Trisha. She's got the doggie bags and can tell you where the trash is outside."

THE ENTRANCE WAS LIKE THE GATE AT THE BACK OF THE San Francisco FBI office but had a guard shack controlling the rolling gate. The two guards were anything but window-dressing.

Muna's comment was quiet and little more than her own mental note. "Glock twenty-seven. Easy draw holster. Quick, but not fast."

James scowled at her as his window lowered. "Easy, tiger. It's not a competition."

"Papers." The man moved his head to take in the four occupants of the vehicle. The tall Indian woman in the back looked over her orange aviators at him as if he should recognize her. He ignored the amateurish move. Even tourists from eastern Toledo tried the same move.

James gave the man his best senior flight attendant snort. "Didn't you mean to say badges? FBI to see Shirley Wicinski." Muna backed him up with her ID wallet.

The guard moved his attention back to Nash.

The hand was a flash with a two-heartbeat exposure ending in a crisp snap.

"One moment." He retreated to the shack. The pause was insignificant before the gate rolled back. He stepped out and pointed. "Park over against the building. Her runner will be right down with a cart to collect you."

The young girl swooped the long golf cart around in an arch as James turned off the engine. He glanced in the rearview mirror. "I could use someone like her on a few of my flights. A pity the sexy jobs always take the good ones."

Muna cracked her door. "Ask her about the seventy-hour weeks she probably works for half your starting pay. Carting functionaries and the occasional star around loses their glamour fast. But usually, these jobs are the foot in the door that never opens."

"Ooh, look at you, miss insightfulness about starter jobs."

Nash growled from the back door. "Ask her about her years of being a junior squint agent while being black and wearing a hijab." She turned and flashed her ID at the young blond behind the mirrored aviators.

The woman beamed. "Is the dog a pet or no pet?"

"It's her world. We just play the bit parts in it."

She patted the front seat next to her. "Dogs sit up front. I'm Vix."

Powder granny crawled into the cart until she could smell the young woman and then hopped onto the spare seat, looking forward.

"Oh, aren't you the crafty one?" She scratched the neck above the tactical vest. "And a snappy dresser, to boot."

Muna climbed in behind the driver. "That's Powder, and I'm Muna. Is Vix short for vixen?"

"Hah. Dad's a stockbroker. The Vix index is how volatile the stock market is. My real name is Veronica or Nicky. But after I got expelled from the fourth school for beating up the bullies, Dad started calling me Vix."

Nash climbed in the back row behind James. "James, our driver, and I'm Nash. You beat up the mean girls?"

The cart rolled as smoothly as a luxury car. "The girls behaved okay. But the jocks and valley jerks picking on the squints and geeks... So I picked on them. Not bad... just a broken leg here and a broken arm there. Word gets around."

Muna glanced back at Nash. "There's a new super girl in town."

Nash laughed. "And James wanted to hire you to be a flight attendant. I'm thinking more about law enforcement or the Marines."

The cart pulled up in front of a bleached tan building. "Can't. I've got a record."

"For bullying the bullies?"

"When I was sixteen, I liked fast cars. Extremely fast cars."

Nash chuckled. "How fast? I drive a Hell Cat."

Vix flattened her lower lip. "Too slow. The Enzo drove nice, but at twelve, it was tired. I liked the LaFerrari more. Better suspension and tighter handling, but the neon pink was a poor choice for three in the morning on the Ventura Freeway. The CHP kind of knew the car. And our neighbor turned into a prick and pressed charges." She flashed a toothy smile. "Too bad her portfolio tanked the next year."

Nash nodded as Powder gave Vix a nose poke to her cheek. "So here you are sucking up to dogs and cruising the studios.

"It keeps me out of trouble with free food and sunshine." She held out her hands with a what's a girl to do sign. "Wicky will call me when you're done. If it's before six, I'll give you the visiting dignitary nickel tour. She's in room one-oh-four on the right."

The classic schoolmarm or spinster librarian looked over her cat-eye glasses. Pulling them off, she let them fall to the extent of the pearl and silver necklace. Her face was impassive as the four filed into her domain. The items on her desk, like photos, trophies, and an autographed football, proved the authority and status of the small woman sitting there.

Nash flashed her ID. "Special Agent Nash Running Bear, agents Muna al-Faragi, Powder, and our escort, James Prentice."

The woman extended her hand as she stood. "Wicky. Nobody can remember if it's Stanley or Shirley now, so Wicky works. Come on in and take some seats. Can I get you anything to drink or eat?" She pulled on the small brooch watch and glanced down. "Ah, Craft is just setting up the late lunch in the commissary."

Nash held up her palms. "We had amazing burritos only an hour ago."

The woman turned and grabbed a computer pad off her desk. Sitting on a side chair, she pulled through the screens. "I believe Gastone mentioned the set dummies…"

"Gastone?"

The woman glanced up. "Oh. Yes. We first met in the Society for Creative Anachronism. Recreating medieval times. He was a fighter, and I was a marshal. He hated Stanislav because I would call him on his armor or hit his opponent below the knee. It was only his light tap distraction move, but it was illegal."

Muna frowned. "We saw the armor. But I don't understand the distraction move."

The woman's hand waved in the air. "His persona was French Cavalier. So he fought Florentine, or with two swords and no shield. He would tap the other guy's leg enough to draw their attention while the killing blow headed for their head."

James chuckled. "The old one-two punch. Jab and haymaker."

"Exactly." She looked at the pad. "Do you have the SKU number for the dummy?"

Nash blinked. "SKU number?"

Wicky looked up. "Yes. Every item, right down to my football, signed by the Gipper, has a unique SKU or Universal Identification Stock number. Some have two if they're used outside of the USA. For the dummies, they would sew a patch onto the back with the number. The prop masters and set dressers call it the prison code because it's the same eight as the federal prison system. Not that I would know anything about prison systems."

Muna cleared her throat in her fist. "Would the tattoo of an eight ball do?"

The leading edge of the computer pad fell softly to her lap as Wicky leaned back in the chair. "Oh my. We thought we had lost the legend to the winds of time." She blinked. "Is the body and head…"

Nash rumbled. "Skinned with actual skin? Yes."

James looked over Powder's head. "What kind of skin are we talking about?"

The three women chorused. "Human."

"No. Seriously…"

The chorus harmonized. "Serious."

21

DUMMY LESSONS

WICKY STEEPLED her fingers over her computer pad. "Eight Ball was a legend in the industry. For one, we used several dummies or mannequins in the filming. Setups, crowd scenes, bar shots, audiences. You name it, and there are probably at least a couple of half-bodies in a shot. Standing, we use dummies-on-a-stick or mannequins. For audiences, the back rows get sprinkled with dummies-on-a-half-shell or just the torso and heads. But for bodies or the homeless, nothing beats the Burbank Eight. They're legendary in an industry that uses the term loosely but not for true legends. Charlie Chaplin, John Wayne, James Dean, and Marilyn make up the hallmark of legends. The Burbank Eight are the notch above."

"What made them so legendary?"

Wicky eyed Muna. "Did you play with Eight Ball?"

Muna twitched as her head retreated on her shoulders. "Play?"

"Pose his hands, sit him up, raise his leg, and it stayed there? Their construction is like no other. Whoever made them was a genius and understood human anatomy. They have bones and joints that work the same way as a person's. And to top everything, they're over fifty years old. Eight Ball, if he weren't a legend before, made status in one five-second shot before they could hide wires or simply CGI what they imagined. Eight Ball took a twenty-four-story fall and crushed a 1937 Chevy Deluxe sedan. Four-camera setup. One focused on the car from the second floor, one from the ground, and one from the next window over. But it was the continuous roll from the camera down the street that was amazing. Film schools use stop-action to examine how the arms and legs are human, not a rag doll. But it was the way the stunt guys strapped the body with an extra two hundred pounds of weight belts, so when he hit, the car crushed to the seats."

James blanched. "Ouch. I know how the guy felt."

Nash pointed. "James is a flight attendant in first class. He spent the last three years getting bodywork from violent air. We missed him."

Wicky twisted her neck in understanding. "What happened?"

"I stepped out of the front galley. When I'd finished hitting walls, floor, ceiling, and passengers, I lay spread across rows eleven and twelve." He pointed to his knee. "My warranty on the new knee is twenty years or two million miles, whichever comes first. The shoulder didn't come with a warranty, just warnings. My seven broken ribs hurt the worst, along with the phone calls from scheduling. They even called when I was in the hospital heading for hip surgery, wanting me to pick up a flip the next day. But we're all good now. And the seventy pounds I gained flying the couch came off in the first two months back."

Wicky blinked twice. "I can get you a job with the stunt crew here. You're already qualified."

The three glared in unison. "No, thanks."

Nash rolled her finger in the air. "So, Eight Ball… do we know what he was doing in New Mexico in an Apollo space suit?"

Wicky shook her head. "We bought a ton of props, sets, and costumes when Burbank cleaned house just before the pandemic. It took us two years just to catalog and absorb all of it into our system. All the properties we didn't think we bought filled two of our soundstages to overflowing. And much of the stuff was useless, falling apart, or left us scratching our heads."

She jerked her thumb toward her desk. "My football. Signed by the Gipper himself and the entire cast team. We don't even stock sports stuff. Buy a few balls, scuff them up, scribble something, and roll film. If one of the cast takes the ball home after, it beats filling the dumpster. Gippy wasn't even a prop. It was a waylaid after-wrap gift. But Ron signed the ball, so we don't even know who it was for. So I got a new toy. My dad was a grip on the movie."

"And Eight Ball...?"

"He was on the manifest, but nobody could find him. We thought Burbank held him back, but then, over the years, it just didn't matter anymore. Otherwise, he might be sitting in the chair you're sitting in. But I know he's not in our system. There's a place-holder for him, but he's not there. So when you release him…"

Nash slowly blinked her acknowledgment. "He can come home to your parlor."

"So, this puts a wrap on your case?"

Nash snorted softly. "Hardly. It just twists the mystery harder. We know who he is now but not who he was. Plus, his presence in the saloon is still in question."

Wicky stood and set the computer pad on her desk. "Well, if we never possessed Eight Ball, we didn't sign him out. So let's go talk to Nate about his errant child." She picked up a walkie-talkie. "Vix?"

"Yes, ma'am?"

"Bring a limo around. We're going hunting on the back lot of Burbank."

The radio clicked twice.

"Anyone need a potty break before we go?"

In the back of the limousine, Muna found the photos on her phone. She quietly handed it over to Wicky.

Wicky smiled at the dummy sitting with a crossed leg on the

edge of the autopsy table. His hand held out Muna's prized original Heman doll.

Wicky passed the phone back. "I don't know what kind of office you have, but I'd at least print out a copy for a photo frame or larger."

"We don't keep trophies from cases, but now that I know who Eight Ball is, I'll make an exception. The boys have had some fun with his adaptive nature. His X-ray has hung on Mike's glow board for a few days now. They'd really like to cut him open to look at the skeleton handiwork. But aren't sure if they could put him back together."

Wicky smiled and leaned in. "I'll make you a deal. You give me Eight Ball, and I'll send you the most trashed sibling, making it easier for your boys to cut open." She presented her hand, and they shook.

Vix drove past the main gate with the extensive line of people waiting to get into the taping of one show or another. She glanced back. "Even when masks were still required, the lines spanned the block overnight. People fly here without reservations or tickets and wait, hoping the shows didn't sell out."

Wicky leaned forward. "Is your sister still working on the reservations?"

Vix's head flicked back and then returned to driving. "Roommate, but yeah, same thing. They have her evaluate the contingent groups for the games. She's got an eye for high-energy contestants."

Wicky's eyebrow rose slightly as she looked at the other three. "An extremely valuable skill."

"They recognize and pay her what she's worth."

Wicky gave a soft burp of laughter. "Yes, dear. I'm paying attention to what you do and how well you do it. And I don't think the stunt guys have noticed you eyeing their wheelhouse, either. We'll bump you up the Associate Producer ladder and get you more pay this fall." She rolled her eyes at Nash. "She's already got her crash bus license and whatever else."

The correction floated back from the front. "It's called a twenty-ton. But it's a restricted class-A driver's license. But I've already drifted a bus and tractor-trailer."

"Yes, dear. Please get us through the gate in one piece."

Vix drifted to a silent stop at the guard. "Mohamad has come to see the mountain."

The guard leaned his curly gray head close to the window. "Good to see you, Wicky. Is this going to be a rowdy tour?"

"No, Jackson. Wrong solstice. We'll all be inside and keep our clothes on... this time. You don't need to speed-dial the police. They'd only laugh at the old woman, anyway."

The man beamed at the humor. "Very good, ma'am. Just checking." As he stepped back, he warned Vix. "Keep it under eighty until after you're out of sight, young lady."

Vix gave him a two-finger salute that didn't turn into a single. Muna watched the shoulders and the young woman constantly checking her mirrors and the cross streets.

The street looked like a familiar residential neighborhood. James chuckled. "Mockingbird Lane."

Wicky nodded. "Stop at the mansion, Vix. We have someone tripping down Munster Lane."

Nash shied her head sideways at James. "The Munsters. As in Herman and Morticia?"

James and Wicky laughed. "Herman, yes. But Morticia was the Addams Family. Herman was married to Lily, played by Yvonne De Carlo."

Wicky flipped her hand out. "And then there was Lee Meriwether in the remake." Her eyes looked at the roof without a roll.

James buzzed his lips. "Nope, Yvonne was the only one. And nobody could ever be Herman. Even as a kid watching the old black and whites, I wondered why Herman was working as a cop in *Car 54, Where Are You?*"

The limousine eased to a stop. "Munster Manor, madam."

The house was an overblown three-story McMansion in vanilla

ice cream with butter brickle trim and door. More of a nineties whore story than a cemetery residence of horror. Wicky shrugged as James looked back. "And the world moves on. Originally built for Hitchcock's Psycho. Then, too perfect to dismantle, so they dressed her up with spider webs and the cemetery, and it became an institution."

James frowned. "But I thought it was on a tour..."

Wicky smirked. "This one moved on. The entire back lot is a nonstop working location. So Universal built another one for their tours. Tourists get to see what they want. It's Hollywood... except it's not. We're in Toluca Lake, and the other end of the studio is in Burbank. Same land different tax structures. So they shoot historical films over there. They tax films with an educational value accordingly lower."

Nash sighed. "It sounds complicated."

Wicky sat back. "Dreadfully. The administration, or pencil pushers who have no direct touch with the industry, is comprised of accountants and lawyers. Even some producers have law degrees. They never passed the bar, but they have the paper. They feel it keeps them out of trouble, and they're right. We can head for the mountain Vix."

"Yes, ma'am."

Nash chuckled and nudged Muna as they turned down the short street. The man wore a black T-shirt and board shorts. He only missed huaraches, pink toenails, and about seven inches.

Muna growled softly. "I bet he doesn't have a stainless-steel spine, either."

Wicky leaned forward. "Don't let the surfer dude's appearance fool you. Those shorts are hiding a pair cast in the hardest iron."

Nash turned with a smile. "We have a friend down in Orange County. With a rude shirt or just irreverent and huaraches, it could pass for Frank. But our guy stands six and a half feet, and this guy..."

Wicky nodded. "Presents like my little brother but wields power way above Walking Tall."

Vix opened the back door and stood at loose attention as the four stepped out.

"And how's my little brother holding up?"

They hugged in the traditional Hollywood, lightly European manner.

"Hell. All I get is hell. You're the bright speck in my month." He turned. "Hi, welcome to Burbank Studios. Nathanial Hawkins. Nate to everyone but my mother. She gets away with calling me Punky."

Wicky pointed in a rapid-fire pistol. "Nash, Muna, James, and Powder. Stay on her good side. She can find the buried bodies."

He waved his own pistol finger among the group. "And this crash meeting is for… a luau?"

Wicky studied him until he calmed into a solemn look on his face.

"I noticed the badges. Who died?"

Wicky braced his arm with her grip. "All these years later, it's who turned up."

"Hoffa?"

"Worse. Eight Ball."

"Oy. The dummy?"

"No. Fabio's twin, the mid… oops. The small person. Yes, the dummy."

He looked around from Nash to James. "Where?"

Nash took out her ID wallet. "First…"

Muna matched her. "We have questions."

22

SIFTING PAPER

THE AFTERNOON WAS CASTING LONGER shadows on the sidewalk. The man pinched the bridge of his nose. "Oy. I should have known this wasn't going to be a drive-by." He looked over their shoulders at the young woman leaning against the limo. "Vix, if you want to go grab a coffee or something to eat, craft is set up in the long room."

She silently gave him her two-finger salute and held her hands out at the limo.

"Nope. It's fine right there. Nobody is going to mess with it."

She turned and strolled off as she whistled the theme song from Mayberry.

Nate rolled his eyes. "She's too young to know that song." He turned and scooped his hand in the air as he walked toward the building's door.

Muna smirked. "Nickelodeon and YouTube are wonderful teachers. I'm finding a whole new appreciation for the silent movie era."

Nash grumbled. "She had a sheltered childhood. Study, pray, and no boys."

Muna rolled her eyes toward the sky. "I'm not that pathetic. Oh, wait. Yes, I was. No television, no movies, and only books my mother approved of."

Nate nodded. "Gurl. Same. College must have been eye-opening."

Muna flattened her lower lip as she pushed it out and vibrated her head. "Not really. I just studied harder and held my head down." She looked up at the man. "I wore a hijab until this last year. Same as my mother."

He opened the door and held it. "Mahsa Amini?"

Muna nodded as she stepped in.

"A lot changed around the world. Conversations people had never broached before became open and gutsy. Iran will have a tough time sticking the genie back in the bottle."

Muna stood to one side as the others entered. "Exactly what my mother said. They can't go back. Too many remember the freedom and open life under the shah."

"Many movies got filmed in many locations, even on the streets of Tehran. Sexy, racy movies. Tehran looked a lot like Paris, but cheaper." He held his hand out. "My office... here on the left."

The office was the antithesis of Wicky's office. Sliding wallboards lined his walls. Each held complicated setup and shooting schedules from soundstages to the back lot and even remote locations. Nash snickered and smirked at Muna.

Muna waved her down. "Yeah, yeah, yeah. His table is bigger than mine. I get it."

"Table?" The man pushed the large desk chair out from behind the desk.

Muna stepped in front of Nash. "When we have a complicated case, I build a table to lay out all the parts or people."

Wicky sat in the large wing-backed leather chair. "You build a table each time?"

Nash folded her hands on top of Muna's head like she was a little sister. "Her office space could pass for a ballroom. During World War II, over fifty people worked logistics in the open office.

They left the space and the large wooden desks. We push them together as we need the area. Sometimes, we can get away with only six desks. Recently, we were using—"

Muna looked through the top of her head but didn't step away from the belittling gesture. "We eventually used a configuration of three deep and four wide. There were nineteen plus two people we needed to get straight and on track. The case became intricately complicated."

Nate mixed his hand around in the air. "So you had a hundred and eighty square feet covered in paperwork and files..." His frown grew deeper. "How do you keep it all straight?" He pointed at his walls. "Each of my panels is a location or series of small locations..."

Muna shook Nash's hands off her head and stepped to the wall. Nash recognized Muna's teaching stance as her hand signaled the large panel. "I like your layout, but it's just markings. What's this movie?"

"It's a low-grade slasher going straight to streaming fill."

Muna slid the panel aside and tapped the next board.

"Urban rom-com."

She stepped back and tapped her knuckle on the board, and laughed. "Space Balls Six? Really?"

He shook his head. Nowhere was such a title written, but he now knew she was fast at taking in the concepts. "Streaming winter fill, and yes, it's a space comedy."

She laughed. "With furries. Which animals?"

He shrugged with a bored droop of one eye. "Who knows? They checked out about a dozen mixed bags. And knowing this producer, he probably has a few of his own personal thrown into the mix. So what's your point?"

Muna moved her flat hand up and down the panel. "Your information is vertical so that you can slide these back and forth. But I spread my information across a plane." She held her hands out and moved them as if they were on her table. "So I use vertical indicators." She taped the space movie board. "This would be... I think I have the gremlin doll, Gizmo. Small, science fiction, and lots of trouble."

She stepped to the next panel. "I have an STL file to print the famous kiss on VE-day—the sailor and the dame. New York's Times Square is romantic. Throw in my King Kong, and you have some comedy."

She pulled the original board back along the track. "Nothing says slasher like Michael Meyers or Freddie Kruger. But I'm kind of partial to Jason and his hockey mask."

Nash stepped over. "You probably remember the bodies out in the desert commune. We used Aquaman for the water researchers, Rah, the Egyptian Sun God for the solar, and the little guy for the wind."

Muna rolled her eyes. "Little guy... sheesh—Thor."

Nash pushed her finger at Muna's shoulder. "No, who was the little Shaolin Priest kid?"

"Oh. Yeah. Before I remembered, the wind got converted to electricity—"

James beamed on the large couch next to Powder. "The last airbender, Aang."

Nate's smile was wonky as he looked at Wicky. "Remind you of anything?"

Wicky burped a chuckle. "Comic-Con, and I'm never going back. But I understand your selections. It's why he uses these boards. Every day, he has dozens of shoots to keep track of. And for you, you look across your table and can instantly see what you're looking for."

Nate sat up and pointed to the other chairs and couch. "But I'm more interested in Eight Ball."

Nash sat in the club chair. Her hands smoothed out along the aged leather, feeling the cracks. "So are we. And what he was doing in the bar."

"Bar?" Nate and Wicky were a two-part harmony.

Nash glanced over at Muna, who held up her palms. "It's your story. I wasn't there."

Wicky rumpled her forehead. "I thought you two work together."

Nash twitched her head. "We do. But she was off punching holes in targets. Her other job for now."

Nate crossed his legs. "This bar…"

"There's a ghost town… well, a wild west sort of town. I suspected you might tell me more about it. It's in the northwest section of New Mexico near a town named… something, something cheater."

Muna had her phone out. "Nasty cheater…" She looked up with a shy smile. "Naschitti. It's north of Yah-Ta-Hey. Which is north of Gallop."

Wicky laughed. "You made that up."

"No. It really is Naschitti."

"No. The Yah-Ta-Hey. That's old black-and-white Indian stuff. John Wayne, Roy Rogers, the forties kind of two Indians meeting." She raised her right hand in greeting. "Yah-Ta-Hey?"

Nash snorted. "This Paiute Indian drove through Yah-Ta-Hey. I would have stopped if I thought any store would have some trinket with Yah-Ta-Hey on it. But not even a gas station to buy fuel and get a receipt with maybe Chevron #147 Yah-Ta-Hey, New Mexico."

Nate grabbed a legal-sized yellow tablet from his desk and sat back down. "How did you spell the cheater thing?"

Muna grinned. "Nas, like in Nasty, then chitti as in *Chitty, Chitty Bang, Bang*. But with an *I* instead of a *y*."

He paused his pen and looked at Nash. "Was there a name or anything for the ghost town?"

"Not even a name over the saloon. The land office had a name, but I didn't take any pictures or write it down. The bank was something generic, like First Mountain Bank or We Have Your Money Bank. Everything vanilla, which is one reason I think the town isn't as old as its appearance."

"Vanilla, how?"

Nash leaned forward. "The town's about five blocks long. The OK Corral is at one end, as it should be, and the white-steepled church is at the other end. So when you look down the main street, there's the church." She held both hands vertical and parallel, facing the end of the street.

Wicky eased onto one elbow. "Where's the bank?"

"In the middle of town. The land office and sheriff's office are across the street from the bank and the saloon."

Wicky gazed over at Nate. "Sound familiar?"

Nate rocked. "John Ford and the Twenties. He established the layout for the western genera before even the talkies took hold with Wayne and Stagecoach."

Wicky held out her finger. "I came up through the ranks. I started the same as Vix's job and worse, to where I am today. All my learning was on the job. Nate was smart and short-circuited that part of the job. He got his degree in the history of cinema before he started the grind. So, you want to know who did what and where? Nate's your boy. Man. Oh crap, what's politically correct these days?"

Muna laughed as she held up her right index finger, crossing the left index. "Don't ask me. I'm Muslim and used to wear a hijab, but I'm addicted to thermal nuclear-flavored pork rinds. So what's correct? I have no clue nor care. Just a little black girl here, and the other stuff? Way over my pay grade."

Wicky looked at Nash and mouthed *pork rinds?*

Nash nodded. "Don't miss the thermal nuclear part. Her bag of choice has a nuclear bomb on the front and is labeled Beyond Scovil. If she opens a bag in the building, everyone's nose hairs get seared to the root. Mine stopped trying to grow back."

Nate held his hands in the time-out formation. "As much as I like the distractions, we keep getting off-topic. Eight Ball. So what was he doing in this… saloon?"

Nash cleared her throat. "Short story? Lying around on his backside."

Nate leaned forward and pinched the bridge of his nose. "The longer story? The one explaining how he was dressed in the pink tutu and holding a purple unicorn."

Nash adjusted in her chair. "It appeared as if he had crashed through the roof and ceiling and landed on a large table and chair. The table crushed down around its two pedestals, smashing seven chairs underneath it."

"And he was in cowboy gear."

"I didn't say that. But he was in what appeared to be a western saloon."

Nate clipped his pen to the notepad. "Well, how did they dress him?"

Nash frowned at Muna. "The experts said it was…?"

"Apollo Eleven. Lunar exploration suit. Probably Lunar Module Pilot Buzz Aldrin's suit. It's a skosh smaller than Neil's."

Nash flattened her lower lip as she nodded and pointed at Muna. "What she said."

"Seriously?"

Nash held up her hand. "Honest Injun. At least, that's what my official report said."

Nate rocked back in his chair and then looked over at Wicky. "You can't make this shit up." He looked back at Nash. "Where is he now?"

Muna coughed in her fist. "Hanging out in autopsy at the San Francisco field office. If the boys are behaving their age, Eight Ball should be in a chill drawer with the other stiffs."

Nate watched Wicky. "And if they aren't behaving?"

Muna rolled her eyes. "I'm sure they're taking photos, and they've posed him everywhere they can be mischievous. Especially at my desk and computer."

Nash snorted. "Dressed in Hello Kitty pajamas."

"With a tactical vest."

The two rolled their eyes.

Nate reached his desk and grabbed his smartphone. Scrolling through his contacts, he thumbed the choice. "Hi, Jason. I can hear you're driving, but there was a western location. The whole town. Blacksmith and boarding down a full John Ford layout to the white-steepled church. It's near a town named Naschitti. North of Gallop, New Mexico. I need any and all information you can have for me by, say, noon tomorrow." He nodded. "Thanks."

As he put the phone back on his desk, he looked back at the doorway. "Hello, Vix."

Everyone turned.

"Craft packed up. They offered me more coffee to go, but I've had too much, anyway."

Wicky nodded and stood. She didn't have to look at her watch. When Craft, the catering for the movie industry, packed up, it was time to go home. Location shoots would start up in four hours for the night shooting. Day shooting would spend the next ten hours revising scripts and reworking shots, and the actors would get their new lines for their breakfasts.

"We're done here for the day. We can screw it all up again tomorrow." Wicky looked at the agents. "What are your plans for dinner?"

Nash and Muna stood. "Our planning ended with meeting you. We've been off the rails ever since."

Wicky looked at Vix. The deadpan face spoke volumes.

Vix nodded. "Where did you have in mind?"

"See if Musso and Franks can squeeze in a party of five plus the dog."

Vix rolled out of the door, and they could hear her talking in the hallway.

Muna pointed at the door as she raised her one eyebrow.

Nate and Wicky both chuckled as Wicky explained. "As an executive producer, my name will be the reservation. But she needs to build the connections to make things happen in this city. In another couple of years, she'll be another one of the more powerful associate producers who is never connected to a script. This is where the sorting hat in Harry Potter came from this town. If you want to wield power, you keep the day job that has you working every day for a paycheck. If you're driven to make movies, you become a showrunner for TV or a producer's or director's assistant for movies. Her life is hell right now, but soon, her life will have the highs when she has a show to work and the depth of despair when there's no work. It's a crazy world from the outside, but inside, it's exciting to watch who's coming up through the ranks." She flipped her finger back and forth between Nate and herself. "We chose the paycheck."

Vix stepped into the doorway. "We have seating in forty."

Wicky turned to Nate. "We'll see you shortly after high noon tomorrow."

"Make it one, and I'll have Craft layout lunch in the old writer's room."

Wicky nodded. "That's a wrap."

23

SIFTING SAND

MUNA, Nash, and Powder sat watching the table, the street, and a park. Past the forty feet of park grass, the ocean stretched to the horizon. If there were surfers, the cliff edge hid them. The early morning sunshine cast hardline palm tree shadows on the grass. The heat on the back of their necks and the freshly mowed lawn smell were strong harbingers of the day to come—summer in Los Angeles.

"Ming wanted to know why we were so close but stayed in Los Angeles last night."

Nash's growl was soft but deep. "Because I wanted to sleep off the Osso Bucco. And why do they still have the nanny tracker still going?"

Muna sipped on her coffee. "Because they worry about us." She peeked at the smile growing on Nash's face before the coffee cup could hide it. "So it wasn't the banana split?"

"Bananas Foster. Not as much ice cream."

Muna peeked at the little girl separating them. She couldn't tell if Powder was sleeping with her eyes open or just staring at the people in the park doing yoga. "Vix didn't seem to have much problem with the meal."

Nash rolled her head to face the younger agent. "How did you eat when you were only nineteen?"

"My mother didn't get her fingers near my mouth. But wow. A dozen oysters, salad, some kind of steak—"

"Diane. It was Steak Diane."

Muna ticked her head in a nod. "With all the trimmings, and then the ice cream piled with whipped cream. I was almost embarrassed for her."

"Why? Because she ate it faster than you? And you didn't have the oysters." Nash glanced over. "I didn't know they weren't halal. Learn something every day."

They followed Powder's lead and sat watching the air and distant sea.

"Okay. Three Santa Monica omelets, one halal, and one chopped in a bowl with no jalapenos. Two wheat toasts, two fruit subs for potatoes, and one veggie mix over the chopped omelet. I'll be right back with fresh coffee. Anything else I can grab, pepper sauce, worst shire sauce, more napkins, extra ice cream, more toast...?"

The three stared at the young woman, who seemed to have said all that in one breath. They ignored the nose ring and three lip studs on only the left side.

Nash cleared her thought. "No thanks. The sauces make the coffee taste funny."

She paused and then held her palm out. "No, the sauces are for the eggs. Oh"—she rolled her eyes—"duh. That's a good one. I'll be right back."

Muna, with her mouth open, turned toward Nash.

Nash pointed a finger at her. "No. Stop. Don't you ever try to mimic the Mach Five mouth. Never. I will suffocate you in your sleep. Then I will hunt down your ghost and haunt you for all eternity."

Muna closed her mouth and studied her food. Powder waited for someone else to start.

Muna's voice was soft as she picked up her fork. "Can I record her and play it for Vix?"

"Don't encourage her. She has her own path to walk. Her model is Wicky. Leave her alone."

The waitress refilled the mugs as they quietly ate. She slid the check under Powder's bowl and left.

Nash burped a soft laugh. "Did you get all that?"

"Ass."

"Are you PMS because you didn't get to shoot this morning? I mean… we can find a range for you."

"I didn't bring my guns."

"Nothing?" Nash frowned in horror over Powder. Powder sensed the movement and turned slightly toward Muna.

Muna leaned forward and muttered into her omelet. "Just my service PPK."

Nash leaned back to the chair. "There. Now I feel safer."

"Ass."

Muna's phone pinged as they walked back to the SUV. She fished it out and read the text. "James is awake and wants to know when breakfast is served."

Nash chuckled as her pocket vibrated. "Persistent little princess, isn't he?" She read her text. "Vix says to show up at eleven if we want a tour."

Muna wiped out the message she was typing and retyped. She waited for the response. "Funny, I would have thought he'd use the middle finger instead of the thumb." She slipped it into her pocket as she opened the driver's door.

"What did you tell him?"

"I told him we ran our five miles on the beach and already got some healthy green slime shakes. And we'd be back in an hour."

"You're getting evil in your old age."

"I learned from the master."

Nash cupped her hands over Powder's ears. "Don't listen to her,

Powder. She'll lead you down the wanton path to Chow Fats, and you'll never be the same again."

James stood, softly bouncing on his toes, next to all their bags. His smile hid in his mustache and beard.

Nash peeked over at Muna. "Did you pack before we left?"

Muna scowled at her bag on the sidewalk. "No…"

As Nash got out, she pointed at the bags and looked over the top of her dark glasses.

He rolled his eyes dramatically behind his Clark Kents. "Oh, girl. Do you think this is the first time I've packed the whole crew's gear? Get over yourself. You wear nothing even halfway interesting. Well… except for the leather pants. Those, I might…"

"You'll need three days in San Francisco. Muna gets a special rate. But you might like the rest of the boutique… It's on the nastier end of Polk Street. The leather bar is next door." She stepped toward the door.

"Already taken care of. And no. I did not get you a receipt. And I need to be at LAX by seven."

Nash swung back and grabbed the two rucksacks. "If it runs late, we'll get you a town car."

James harrumphed as they loaded the back. "Limos. Such a waste of space and privacy when you're all alone."

"Don't be nasty."

"I'm just sayin' girlfriend."

VIX TOOTED THE TINY HORN AS MUNA PARKED IN THE lot. She looped around as they got out. "Does the little one need to powder her nose before we get buried in fantasy land?"

Nash looked down at Powder. "The tree is over there with the only grass for an hour or more. Everything from here on out is an expensive prop, and they'll get mad if you pee or poop on it."

Powder old lady limped to the tree and squatted for a couple of heartbeats. She pranced back and climbed up next to Vix. The girl got a nose on the cheek as the others took their seats.

The Surry-topped cart slipped past the large buildings. "These are all soundstages. They tied up this big one for a few years. They built a scale model of the Enterprise for the original Star Trek inside. Afterward, they had to decide whether to tear out an end wall or take the model apart. They finally opted to wash it with scalding hot water and blow-dry it with flaming torches." She turned and quietly drove past the twelve-foot-long model of the original Enterprise NCC-1701. "It shrank a lot. And then they got worried because they couldn't find two workers." She shrugged. "They were red shirts."

Vix and Muna giggled as they took the next corner.

James called out from the back. "I need a better picture of the Enterprise. I have a family of Trekkie Junkies. They'll love the joke."

Vix slowed into a U-turn.

<hr>

"AND THIS BRINGS US TO THE END OF THE LITTLE CART. It's not legal for the street. So we're back in the limo. Does anyone need a potty break? The boys are on the left, and us ladies..."

Wicky pulled open the back door as they pulled up. Muna giggled. "Get in if you want to live."

Wicky chuckled. "Best line he ever delivered."

They parked in front of the building at 12:59. Nash and Muna both checked their watches. James laughed. "This is when ground control calls the cockpit and tells them to hold for ten. But it's twenty-eight minutes until they release us. Even though the door closed on the button."

Wicky frowned as they got out. "I never got what you do besides look pretty."

He smiled. "Thirty-three years as a flight attendant for American."

Her mouth made the ouch. "Rough job."

Nash slid out. "Especially when you get thrown all over the cabin and passengers in severe turbulence. He was in the repair shop for three years."

Wicky examined him up and down.

He rolled his eyes. "New knee, hip, and arm socket. I'm good for another twenty million miles."

Over lunch, they worked.

"Transportation got back to me about your ghost town." Nate pointed at Nash. "They confirmed your suspicion. They built it during the height of Westerns in the early sixties. If you knew what to look for, you could have noticed the boards with names on them were interchangeable. Permanent names like gold-leafed words painted on windows are probably generic, like banks, dry goods, and land offices. People expect to see them and don't care who the name over the door is."

Nash put down her fork and dabbed at her mouth. "Thick dust covered everything in the saloon. Even Powder didn't trigger on any smells or sense of anyone having been there in a long time."

Wicky pointed with her fork. "What about the people who found the body?"

"We accompanied the deputy who had processed the find, and Powder had smelled him. He'd walked everywhere the new people had. But then, that's surmising. Some days, I don't know how her mind works."

Muna patted her mouth. "Any idea who had rented the dummy and was filming?"

Nate chewed on his lasagna and pointed his fork at Wicky.

Wicky shook her head. "In the great move, you unloaded a lot of your trash, but we never received Eight Ball. So I'm guessing this production pre-dated the move." She pointed her fork at Nate. "So the Eight Ball is in your court. So to speak."

Nate held his hands over his chest. "Ouch. Straight to the heart. You only want Eight Ball for your office collection."

"Damn straight, kid. I'll sit him in the corner wearing one of Stan Laural's old suits. Then I can blame every fine mess on him."

Nate held his phone to his head. "Pam, find out when we last rented out the set dummy named Eight Ball. No SKU number, only his name. I'm in a luncheon, but I need the information as soon as you can get your computer to spit it out." He nodded. "Thanks." He placed it face down on the table, where it vibrated every so often.

Muna swallowed and sipped on her coffee. "Would your records also tell you where Eight Ball came from? He's kind of unique."

Nate pushed the plate an inch away from him. "Because of the leather skin?"

Nash drooped her eyes. "Because the leather skin is a tanned human skin."

Both prop managers froze.

Wicky frowned. "Human? You weren't kidding before?"

Muna nodded. "Because of the tanning, we couldn't run any DNA tests. Any fingerprints are long gone now because of the wear and glazing on the fingertips. I've run searches on thousands of tattoos, but the Eight Ball was ridiculous. In the prison system of the United States, I got over seven million hits. The most I could restrict was barely under a million. Evidently, it's a popular tattoo."

Wicky studied Nate. The man was pinching the bridge of his nose. "Thoughts, young man?"

James glanced at his watch and held it up to Nash. Tapping the face of the watch, his eyes became enormous in the Clark Kents. "It's always this way. Just when it's getting interesting, duty calls."

Wicky frowned. "What's going on?"

Muna held up her phone. "James has to be at LAX to catch his flight." She screwed up her face at Nate. "You don't happen to have a helipad big enough for a Black Hawk, do you?"

Wicky pulled out her phone and dialed. "What time do you need to be there, dear?"

"Seven thirty would cut it really close."

She nodded. "Vix, can you get James to LAX by seven?" She

nodded and stared at Nate. "Can she borrow your car? She needs to take the canyons and something, something."

He fished the Porsche key fob out of his pocket. "But bring it right back and stick it on the charger."

Muna stood. "But he'll need his luggage out of the rental. I'll bring the SUV back."

After the hugs and goodbyes, Wicky and Nate sat with Nash and Powder in silence.

"Eight Ball, Nate?"

Nate held out his palm. "I'm thinking, I'm thinking."

Pulling his phone off the desk, he thumbed through and pressed the contact. Sighing, he pushed the green icon.

"Hi. It's Nate. Is Celeste still here?" He listened as he snuck furtive peeks at Wicky. "Okay. Clear a couple of hours for her tomorrow morning. No. More important. She has some explaining to do to the FBI. No, the kind with real badges, guns, and a dog from Washington, D.C. Good. Ten o'clock it is. I'll bring them over."

MORE SAND, MORE SIFTING

POWDER TURNED her head toward Nash.

Nash smacked her lips. "Yes. It looks exactly like yesterday. But I think the woman in the blue spandex wasn't here yesterday."

Muna snickered. "The boys have been having way too much fun. I think they need a large serial murder."

Nash looked over Powder to study the smaller agent looking at her phone. The angle was acute, but Nash could see the images were moving. "How much fun?"

"Just a second. Let me start it over." She fingered the screen and passed the phone over. "I think they forgot Chips and Baby are still over in the corner and watching everything." Muna sipped on her mug. "I think Chips put the montage together."

In a video, Nash watched the two men dressing up the dummy in different costumes. As they expected, Hello Kitty pajamas and Day of the Dead scrubs dominated. The tactical vest changed from a level two to an old Navy plate flak jacket from, Nash guessed, World War II. The source of such, she had no doubts. She paused the video and showed it to Muna. "Where did they find a three-piece suit in plaid?"

Muna rolled her eyes. "Hiding in the back of Oz's closet since he was twenty?"

They peered up at the enormous shadow cast by the serving tray. The waitress popped open the stand with one hand and set the tray down. Without uttering a word, she delivered everything exactly as they had ordered the day before. She filled the mugs and set the carafe on the table. From her apron pocket, she pulled out a small bag and laid it in front of Muna.

Taking up the tray, she closed the stand and left.

Muna held up the small bag. The image of the nuclear bomb was familiar. She had just never seen a one-ounce bag of pork rinds before. She turned to look back into the interior of the restaurant. The waitress wasn't obvious. "I'll be dipped…"

"When did you mention rinds yesterday?"

"I didn't—" Muna frowned at Nash. "—That I remember."

THE TRUCK AHEAD OF THEM LOOKED LIKE A STANDARD moving van. But from what Nash could see, down the side of the trailer was as blank white as the conventional tractor with an over-sized sleeper. Muna pointed at the familiar union symbol of the twin horses. They both smiled at the rest of the large bumper sticker: *Transportation. We put the move in movies.*

Nash rolled her head over to Powder and scratched under her neck and jaw. "I remember Mina telling me the Teamsters walked out in solidarity with the writers, even though they had just signed a new contract. I didn't get it then." She pointed at the bumper sticker. "But I do now."

"From what I've read, it only takes one union to walk out to bring everything to a screaming halt." Muna glanced over as the big rig eased forward through the gates. "No writers, no speeches, no Emmys, or Oscars."

She rolled her head back to look at the large guard. "Um… Nate….?"

The man laughed and glanced at his watch. "You're late FBI. They've been holding doughnuts and coffee for you for over an hour. Park over there in the yellow striping. They're sending a cart down for you."

The blonde's face had more miles than the perfectly pulled-back high ponytail. The sleeveless sweatshirt Nash would have expected more on Frank Pounds than an older woman driving a shuttle cart.

"They told me you also had a K-9…"

Muna and Nash softly snorted as they climbed into the backseat. Finished with her business, Powder raced around the SUV and scrambled up into the seat next to the driver. Her nose pointed forward—all business.

Nash settled back and crossed her arms. "That's her signal she's ready. You didn't get a kiss because she didn't approve of your cologne, soap, or shampoo. But she didn't climb in back here, so I'm assuming she approves of the Ramones sweatshirt. I'm Nash, this is Muna, and the princess is Powder. We all carry badges. But then, you already knew about us."

Nash and Muna both clutched the metal rails tightly as the woman mashed the gas pedal. This wasn't Vix, but a woman who clearly controlled her own destiny. A glance between Nash and Muna carried their mutual understanding. This was not someone to be trifled with. More than likely, the woman stood higher on the proverbial food chain than the production assistants they expected to schlep them to their meeting. "I set us up in the executive screen room. A few other people who need to hear and understand the history will join us." She glanced back. "I hope you don't mind."

Muna distractedly thumbed through some more photos Chips continued to upload to Muna's nasty girl room. "Federal or local law enforcement?"

The cart lost power as the woman glanced back with a frown. "Why would…?"

"Just asking." Muna glanced up. "Tis better to ask than to be blindsided in court. Deklin Steel. *People's Choice*. I believe he referenced *On the Waterfront*, who paraphrased Shakespeare when he quoted Brutus in *The Tragedy of Julius Caesar*."

The blonde squinted her left eye as her right studied Muna. "A filmophile?"

Nash vibrated her head. "Compulsive researchist beyond anything you could guess."

The cart rolled. "So what did you find on my pseudo uncle?"

"Uncle?"

As the woman glanced back, Nash studied the skin on the back of her neck. The crinkled, loose skin the face-lifts and neck tucks never seem to remove.

"Valentine Diego." She snapped another peek back with a frown. "Isn't he why you're here? Figuring out who Eight Ball really was?"

Muna's thumbs typed as she glanced up. "Valentino. As in Rudolf Valentino?"

"No. Valentine. As in *My Dearest Valentine*. As in Lieutenant Valentine Diego of the Headhunters of New Guinea fame." She glanced back. "Look, you can talk to your phone, or you can hold your panties for a few minutes more and learn everything about Val you never thought you wanted to know."

She swung the cart around a corner and straight down a ramp into an underground parking. "Movieland. Where hopes and dreams come to die or soar."

As they climbed out, Nash smiled. "I'm guessing you're Celeste and not the PA schlep of the day."

The woman snorted. "Oh, honey. I stopped being a production assistant the day I met Betsy Dorfman. It was also the day she became Bet and began working her wiles to become one of the most loved and feared Executive Producers in Hollywood." She scooped the air with her hand. "Come on up and pray the fall guys didn't hog all the doughnuts."

The wide hall had tables decked with doughnuts, bagels, coffee, water, juice, and fresh fruit. Muna chuckled as she leaned close to Nash. "Ming must have loaned them Chef."

Celeste held out her hand and arm. "Grab anything you want, and we'll be in the theater through the doors. I need to check with the postproduction before we get started. We only found out about all this last night." They watched as the woman said hello and touched arms and shoulders of the various people while she passed through the doors.

Nash growled quietly. "Remind you of anybody?"

Muna leaned over and picked up a small plate. "I think we've found Felix's mother."

"Don't let the blond hair and cute ponytail fool you. She's more like his grandmother."

Muna peeked up at the door and then smiled at Nash. "It's Hollywood."

The seats rivaled most lounge chairs in living rooms across the land. The noted difference was the drink holders looked suspiciously like they may have started at ashtrays. But the wide arms of the leather-clad seats were flat and held plates squarely. Nash eyed the area and dark shadows of rings in the leather and suspected other kinds of drinks from bygone eras. After all, it's Hollywood. Land of plastic surgery, movies, and consumption of other hedonistic traits.

The era-stained arms of the lodge seats didn't pass the super nose's notice. Powder sat stiff-legged in the middle of the seat.

"Good morning. Sorry for getting a late start, but we gathered even more information and clips as we came here. Most of you are used to filming changes happening after the board gets snapped and called." She licked her lips as she looked around, rolling her one eye at the chuckling crowd. She pointed at one man. "Hey, Hank. How did production go on Wednesday? I heard the writer kept feeding you new lines while they strapped you into your harness."

Several people laughed as he chuckled. "She was still screaming at me as I passed the nineteenth floor."

Celeste shot her finger gun at him as she winked. "Not bad for a four-story building. Keep working on it. I expect the punch line to be up to the thirty-first floor by the Christmas party at the Nakatomi Plaza."

The crowd responded with a *Yippy Ki-Yay motherfucker* cheer and laughed.

Nash frowned at a chuckling Muna, who waved her down and mouthed *later*.

Celeste smiled as she waved down the noise. "As you can tell, most of you have connections to action movies and stunts. Which is why you're here. Most of this presentation we pulled together to release before the history group. Current events sped up the time-line. So, what you will see here today is more of the rush as opposed to a finished film. For our special guests from outside our industry, rushes mean the raw films from the day's work. They let us see how the shooting went, how the acting succeeded or didn't, or if the stunt and its weeks of staging and practice turned out. The term comes from the film being pulled from the camera, rushed to the developing room, and then spliced into a presentation. This very room has been the location where generations of people viewed many rushes shot here on this lot." She held wide her two hands. "Welcome to our history."

She peered toward the back. "J. J.? Are we there yet, or do I need to tell jokes about actors showing up at the wrong locations?"

"Five more minutes... blame the grips."

Celeste winced. "More like the Teamsters. Alright. So let's play questions and answers. Who knows the formation date of the Stuntmen's Association of Motion Pictures?

The crowd roared back *1961*.

Celeste chuckled. "Looks like we might have a few members here today. Raise of hands only. Who knows the first two men and for whom they doubled?" She scanned the sea of arms and pointed.

The man shifted in his seat. "Loran Janes was McQueen's

double, and Dick Geary worked with Robert Vaughn. Do I get an extra cookie?"

Celeste's eyes became enormous. "There were cookies? And I didn't get one?" The laughter was family.

"Those Teamsters grazed through before we got here." The crowd laughed harder.

Celeste's head ticked up to look toward the back. She nodded. "Final answer, and it leads us to today. Who was the first cowgirl in the association?"

Several arms rose, but only one female. Celeste smiled. "Jamie?"

"Barbara Stanwyck for breaking her arm and hip while filming The Big Valley."

Celeste rocked. "Westerns. Always dangerous to stunt actors, actors, actresses, and beasts alike. But today's example started many years before." She pointed toward the back. "Enjoy your history. We'll talk in a few."

The lights dimmed as the familiar choppy black-and-white countdown started on the screen.

25

HISTORY

THE FILM FLICKERED, visually crackled, and popped through the expected countdown from five. The narrator's droning voice was all too familiar as the monotonous soundtrack to every dull history lesson in school.

A propeller fighter plane streamed smoke from the engine compartment. Thin, dark gray smoke turned blacker as the aircraft sank from the sky into the lush jungle below.

"Another pilot seeks refuge in the deep jungles of Papua New Guinea. A haven from the savage Japanese."

The film jerked to show a pilot with a torn and stained uniform smiling at the camera. He stands supported between two dark natives wearing only a bit of clothing near their crotches. Spears in their hands enhanced the threatening look, except for their smiles.

"Here, we see our stalwart pilot with his saviors. Cannibals who inhabit the jungle and hate the Japanese. Although he broke his leg and one arm in the plane crash, a few months home, and he'll be none the worse for wear. Smile, Mom, he's coming home to visit."

The screen was changed to a superior film, but it was still dated. The artist sits on a teepee ladder as he paints the white detail on the nose art of a fighter plane. Turning, he holds out his hand at the art depicting a native head with a broken bone under the head.

"Port Moresby, New Guinea. Sergeant Stevens paints the eightieth squadron's war patch on the nose of a brand new Lockheed P-38 Lightning. The fighter squadron honors the New Guinea headhunters who saved their pilots from the Japanese. Keep up the good work, Sergeant."

The screen darkens in transition to a young man on crutches making his way down a gangplank. His hat was tipped back on his head, and the smile beamed.

"Two days before VJ day, Lieutenant Valentine Diego got shot down a second time in New Guinea, but not before he splashed two more Jap Zeros. Bringing his total kills to twenty-three. You deserve a rest, Lieutenant. And we thank you for your service."

The quality of the film changed a little, but the image was desert badlands. The stagecoach rounded a bend in the road as the cowboy riding shotgun kneeled on the seat next to the driver and shot at the gang of cowboys chasing them. A close-up of the gang leader shows him standing in his saddle and taking careful aim at the shotgun rider.

Firing, the close-up changes to watching the coach as the shotgun rider's arm throws back, and he falls over the side of the stagecoach.

The film cuts to see the stagecoach drive on and the body of the dead shotgun rider lying in the dirt. A moment later, the criminal gang thundered past the body.

The movie fades to a sepia-toned western title with the date of the movie and the name of the character.

As the title block fades, a different movie fills the screen.

Leather-jacketed riders drove several motorcycles. The clips are short and focused on a single rider. A fight breaks out between rival gangs, and most of it plays across the screen. Fading, the title block and the character's name replace the action in the 1953 movie.

The fade opens with the roar of racing cars, replacing the title block. Three cars are neck and neck through the countryside. The close-ups show the actors in half-helmets and goggles. The one character looks back to see where the other race cars are—sending a soft chuckle through the audience.

Nash leans toward Muna. "The driver is Italian. He ripped off his rearview mirror and threw it into the bushes."

Muna giggled at the old joke.

As the three cars squeeze to navigate the turn, the outside car veers off the racecourse, flipping and tumbling into a tree. As the camera angle changes, the car bursts into flames.

The title block now contains the movie title, the character, and a description of the broken bones.

The fade-in follows a wagon with three cowboys being chased by some Indians on horseback. As the wagon drives around a curve, an Indian standing on the top of a large, towering boulder draws his bow and arrow. A cowboy in the back of the wagon shoots him with his rifle, and the Indian, wearing nothing but a breechclout, falls from the high rock.

The title block now displays the hospital stay duration and the list of broken bones caused by the wrongly positioned mattresses.

More movie clips were of falls from horses, out of windows, from a moving train, car, truck, wagon, and stagecoach. Fight clips were of hits to the face, body, arms, and back. Weapons included fists, breaking chairs, a bat, pool cues, boards, and even a frying pan. Everything sounded real, but the broken bones and injuries lists reinforced it wasn't all fun and games.

With each list came various groans and knowing nods from heads in the audience.

Muna leaned over toward Nash. "Sorry for my whining about only getting pistol-whipped…"

Nash snorted. "And getting blown up."

"And really shot…"

The man in front of them glanced back with a frown of curiosity. Nash wiggled her eyebrows, and he turned back around.

A soft cheer rose as the clip opened on a wide view of five chariots racing. The last of the race finished and faded into the title block of the three actors and combined broken bones and recovery times.

The block faded into a western saloon.

Eleanore clutched at the cowboy as she sank to her knees. Her hands slide down his back until she hangs from his belt and gun belt. "Don't go out there, Henry. They're nothing but killers. There's nothing out there for a good-hearted man. Only death."

Henry pushes his white hat back with his thumb as he turns slightly to provide a quartering shot of his squared jaw. "Eleanore, nobody else is going to save this town. So I'm it. I don't like it. You don't like it. But some days, a man has to do what a man has to do. It's his lot in life."

She stifles a sob as she looks up. "But those notches on Chance's belt aren't from picking blackberries. He's a born killer and pure evil through and through." She moves her grip on his belt to only her left hand. The right brings her kerchief and smelling salts to her nose as she turns, slumping until she sits on the floor. "If you go out there, I'll be a widow before the clock strikes noon. How will I live the rest of my life?"

The camera moves in for a close-up of her weeping face and holds.

She sniffed with a heaving chest. Her exposed upper cleavage surges.

The cowboy crashed his way through the swinging doors of the saloon. As the doors bang against the walls, the man takes the last steps to the edge of the wooden sidewalk. He pauses and looks both ways along the deserted street. His right hand eases down and back to rest on the handle of his six-shooter.

He steps down the single step from the sidewalk and porch. The horse neighed in agitation. The distinct sound of a lever-action rifle clicked from above and behind him.

Spinning, he draws and fires at the hombre in the black hat and thick bandito mustache. The man chokes as he grabs his chest and falls through the railing—breaking it as he falls to the street below. A large woof of dust explodes around the body. Tipping his white hat back on his head, the cowboy spins his pistol on his finger and slips the weapon back into the holster hanging low on his belt.

The scene fades to an older woman sitting in a director's chair.

"Valentine Diego was a World War II ace who survived crashing two of his P-38 Lightnings in the jungles of New Guinea. He rose in the Screen Actors Guild when a bit-part actor doing his own stunts was common. Throughout his career, Valentine spent over half a year in hospitals recovering from over seventy-three broken bones. Those included his spine, skull, and neck along with ribs, arms, and legs."

The camera pulled back to reveal a dummy sitting next to her. The tuxedo-clad dummy held out a martini glass.

"But many people fail to recognize his creation of the Valentine set dummy. This lifelike dummy, with its lifelike movement and posable structures, is his legacy and most significant contribution to the film industry he loved and gave his life and body to. I'm Bet Dorfman. Thank you for watching this piece of movie history."

The final title block was a memorial to Betty Dorfman, which faded into a memorial to Valentine Diego.

As the lights rose, two set dressers moved four director chairs onto the stage, with accompanying side tables set with bottles of water.

Celeste strode across the stage. "I'd like to invite our special guests from the Federal Bureau of Investigation to join me up here on the stage, please." She pulled a small sheet of paper from her pocket. "Senior Special Agent Nash Running Bear, Special Agent Muna al-Faragi, and Very Special Agent Powder." She started clapping, and the audience joined in as the three walked down the side aisle and mounted the stairs.

She held her hand out at the three. "We, Hollywood, and especially the stunt community owe these three a debt of gratitude.

They not only found Eight Ball but will also bring him home where he belongs."

As the clapping subsided, she turned to the three. "Please, take a seat. I'm sure everyone here would like to know what you can tell us about finding Eight Ball."

Nash sat and leaned over so Powder could kiss her on the cheek. She knew it also looked like Powder was whispering in her ear. She pursed her mouth in an *O*, nodded, and sat back up as she winced. "As you know, because it's in every movie and television show involving cops or the FBI..." She glanced over at Powder. "Or, as my partner reminded me, we cannot comment on an ongoing investigation."

"But...?"

Nash gaped at the dog, who had turned her head away from her as if to say she was taking zero responsibility for anything being said. The crowd laughed. Nash winced as she scratched the side of her head and watched Powder. "But maybe if we share information in a quid pro quo sort of fashion..."

Powder glanced back at Nash and then studied the ceiling, which caused even more laughter. Nash rolled her eyes in more of a silent movie style of overacting and then smiled at Celeste. "How about if we start with this? There is what appears to be a ghost town in the northwest corner of New Mexico. But we have some information indicating it was constructed as a freestanding set for filming westerns. Having been there and looking at how flat and hard the main street is, as well as it is the only street..."

Celeste pinched the bridge of her nose as she thought. "Anybody know about this place?"

"Is it north of Yah-Ta-Hey?"

Nash watched the man as he stood... and stood... and straightened to his full height. The guy seemed more like a linebacker at a basketballer's height.

"Yes. North of Yah-Ta-Hey. Do you know it?"

His head dipped pragmatically. "Intimately. My daddy helped

build it, and I've worked on a few movies filmed out there. Just before the next town north, there's a large flat rock, and you turn west there. Then, at the post turtle rock, you head north into the box canyon. What's the question?"

Nash smiled. "You just answered four of the nine questions we had. If you can stay behind and fill in the blanks about whom your father worked for and when, it will make my report sound a lot better. My bosses like it when I can show that I did my homework."

The man nodded but kept standing. "Is that where you found Eight Ball?"

Nash smirked, a small nod at Celeste. "Yes. He was goldbricking in the saloon."

The man rocked with a chortle. "Yeah, a lot of dummies end up in saloons." He raised his hand above his waist and then realized how silly it looked. "Can I ask? Main saloon or in the gambling hall area?"

Nash bobbed her head. "Yes. I can tell you've been there. Yes. Away from the bar, so I guess it would be the casino area."

"Yeah. They built it large so it could be dressed and used for several distinct sets. Was he in western togs or regular modern street clothes?"

Nash studied Muna, sitting stoically in her chair. Muna peered back and shoveled her hand out toward the man. "You were the senior agent on location. Answer the man."

Nash burped a small laugh at Muna's change to mommy or senior agent. She shook her head.

"No. Neither. As best as we can put together with the people who created the suit, they outfitted him in an Apollo 11 lunar EVA suit. The whole rig—with the life support module on the back, with seven hours of support still left on the meter."

A banty rooster of an older redhead stood up. "Um… I hate to interrupt…"

The tall guy turned and glided his hand slowly through the air. "Go ahead, Gary. I was done." And sat to make his point.

Nash smiled at the grace of the younger giant of a man. Looking at the freckled redhead going gray, she nodded out her chin.

"Go ahead, Gary."

He pulled and adjusted his belt. "I know you're not one of us movie people, but how was the set dressed? I'm assuming there weren't any crew around…"

"No. No crew around. It seemed like nobody had been there for many years. The dust was almost opaque, which I know from personal experience takes a long time in the desert. But it was inside. I don't know much about set dressing, but it appeared like he crashed through the roof and landed on a gambling table, smashing it and the chairs. So maybe the set was for a cowboy movie or something like that."

The man dramatically tipped up his chin and head. "Spacemen and cowboys… Yup. I've never seen that mixed metaphor in a movie before." He gazed around with rolling eyes, gathering chuckles and a few laughs.

"Care to fill me in? There seems to be an inside joke here."

26

EIGHT BALL IN THE SIDE POCKET

THE GREEN AWNING out front had torn, worn out, and was beyond serving any purpose except as the obvious landmark it provided. As they found a parking spot across the street, Nash gave Celeste a hard look. Looking back at the awning, she then doubled the hardness of her stare.

Celeste had tossed her ponytail and laughed. "Trust me. If this isn't the best Chinese food experience you've ever had, I'll pay for dinner."

The feeling of the glass display at the front counter was one of Nash and Muna both wanting to call the health department. Nothing was dirty or even dusty. It was just a sense of not being fresh, shiny, and spotless. The old man with the seven hairs combed over the top of his tan head nodded sleepily to acknowledge they had entered.

Muna held up her four fingers. "Qǐng sì gè."

The man's drooped eyelids hid most of his eyes as he looked back at the door for the fourth person. Powder stood up with her front paws on the glass. Her badge was obvious. The man's head made half a nod up and back down.

He stood from the tall stool, picked up three menus, and held his naked arm out from his worn white wife-beater T-shirt as he shuffled his half-slippers. The hang of his pants took the shape of what used to be a more robust man, now gone too old and moving older.

Six-foot-high walls separated each table from prying eyes. The half-walls stopped two feet above the floor. However, the deep brown stain or paint lent a somber and even older feel to the restaurant.

"When did they first open?"

The old man stopped at an opening in the walls and held out his hand. "Nineteen twenty-two. We open late on Christmas day. No lunch before one. You no come early." He silently held out the three menus.

Moments later, another man shuffled in wearing the same uniform, if it could be called such, and left three cups and a pot of tea.

Celeste never touched the menus. "You can look at the menu or just order what you like anywhere else." She looked at Muna. "You can order in your Mandarin if you want. I've heard people order in Thai, Tagala, Cantonese, and even in Japanese." She pointed over her shoulder. "Little Tokyo is across the street. During World War Two, my father was in the FBI. They lined the buses up out front to take the Japanese to Manzanar. Some of the Japanese snuck in here in the back. Nobody asked if someone in here was Japanese or Chinese. They were in an old, established Chinese restaurant, so everyone was Chinese. Everyone knew it was a chickenshit roundup, even my dad. He ate here often, and we became friends with everyone."

Muna squinted one eye. "The t-shirts…"

Celeste snorted softly. "The worn wife-beaters, the oversized work pants cinched with too-long belts, and the slippers?" She shook her head. "Hollywood could take pointers from these guys. They have plenty of money to buy a new awning, but then the hipsters would come and expect a nicer place. This way, they go over to Little Tokyo and leave the café to those who know."

Muna nodded. "Chow Fat in San Francisco has a similar feeling. You almost never see non-Asians eating in there. They don't wear wife-beaters, but some of the white shirts are so worn they're almost see-through."

"What do you like to eat?"

"I'm halal, so chicken. My favorite is double mushroom and the sweet and sour if I need the sugar rush."

Celeste looked at Nash. "Halal also?"

Nash laughed. "Everything above roadkill is halal enough for me. Powder likes chicken or beef and vegetables, but no broccoli. It gives her gas."

A new old man shuffled into the cubical. His left hand curled around a small pad of white paper. The right held a pencil. "You know what you want?"

Celeste held her palm up and rattled off a firehose load of Cantonese. The man pushed the pencil around on the pad as he turned and shuffled back out of the gap.

Muna raised one eyebrow. "Those home-schooling lessons have been paying off. I'm impressed."

Celeste chuckled. "Our housekeeper and mother's helper was Japanese but spoke Cantonese. She also spoke enough French to help me through high school. But I grew up speaking Cantonese, Japanese, and English. My mother tried to teach me Oklahoman, but it didn't stick."

Nash smirked. "And how much trouble did you just order us?"

"A lot more than we can eat. But we take no boxes to go. Everything left goes into go-boxes, and then they deliver it out the back door. They probably feed as many on the streets as they eat here. They've been feeding the neighborhood since before World War Two."

"That's got to get expensive, even if it's just the leftovers. The clamshells alone..."

Celeste pointed at the ceiling. "The casino and the girls upstairs help cover all the goodwill."

Muna laughed and stuck her fingers in her ears. "Na, na, na, na, da, da."

Celeste rocked in agreement.

Nash looked out of one eye while pouring tea for the three of them. "So, getting back to Eight Ball. Did you know Valentine?"

"No. By the time I knew about Eight Ball, he was Eight Ball. I only got the back story working for Bet Dorfman."

"I get they call the dummy Eight Ball because of the eight-ball tattoo, but I don't understand the... or any pool ball for a tattoo. Did he shoot a mean game of pool?"

Celeste leaned away from the table as the waiter brought in the five dishes and bowls.

The waiter brought in one last bowl and placed it in front of Powder. "The cook make you his dog's favorite dinner. Chicken, beef, and stir-fried vegetables with some rice. You enjoy, and maybe you go tell cook you like." He smiled at Celeste and the others and left.

Muna's eyes were enormous. "Now I wish Felix were here to do a proper tribute to this meal. What is all this?"

Celeste picked up one bowl, spooned in some rice, and then moved to something looking like a stir-fry. "Everything is halal. The protein will be chicken or tofu. There is nothing exotic in the dishes, simply good solid home cooking they would have gotten in Taipei or Hong Kong." She pointed at another dish with the back of her serving spoon. "That one looks like what you'd call double mushroom, but it's more like four or five different mushrooms and some..." She leaned closer and frowned. "... Bamboo shoots, celery sprouts, baby corn, and chicken. Save some for me."

Nash pointed at Powder's bowl. "Go ahead. It's family style. And I'm not tucking in your napkin. So eat neatly."

Powder nibbled at the bowl.

Celeste put down her bowl and picked up her chopsticks. "Now, about the ball. If you're writing or drawing it, what shape is it?"

Muna shrugged her shoulder as she chewed and rolled her eyes. She stabbed at her cheek with her chopsticks and hummed. "A zero or oh."

Celeste poked her nose as she chewed. "A zero. So we have an eight and a zero."

Nash rolled her finger in the air as she chewed. "Eighty."

Celeste raised her eyebrows as she rocked with a nod. "But it's what the eighty stands for."

Nash rested her hand on the edge of the table as she worked on something. "You mentioned his being a pilot during World War Two. So I guess it's his squadron number."

"Right. The eightieth squadron flying out of Papua New Guinea. They earned the nickname Headhunters because of their close ties with the native cannibals, also referred to as headhunters. The native headhunters hated the Japanese. So if an American crashed in the jungle, the native tribes took care of them."

Muna stabbed the air with her chopsticks. "Valentine. He's the guy hobbling down the gangplank in the newsreel? He lost two planes?"

Celeste bobbed her head. "At the end of the war, he crashed deep in the jungle, and I guess pretty banged up. The tribe who found him nursed him back to health and then brought him out to civilization. But while he was recovering, he watched the person tattooing the tribesmen. He chose the eight ball as the symbol for the eightieth and sketched it out for the tattooist. And then he lay there while the man copied the drawing. I've seen videos of how they do those crude tattoos. We're talking about a sharp thorn stuck on the end of a stick. It's an amazing talent."

Muna shuddered. "I've seen those videos. Even a simple pictograph takes hours. Excruciating long hours. One videographer was getting a tattoo in Africa somewhere. And he was basically chewing on coca leaves. High as a kite, but still..."

Nash pushed her bowl away and took a sip of water. "Okay. So we now understand the tattoo and the significance of the eight ball." Her eyes rose, and she looked through eyelashes at the blonde.

Celeste's mouth drew tight. Her upper lip curled in, and the white edge of her lower teeth showed as she bit into the tough question she knew was coming. Her voice was little more than her breath. "The skin…"

Nash gently rocked. "The skin."

Muna dropped her fist to balance on the tip of her braced index finger as her voice rose into the strident. "No. I want the entire story. We're not talking about some fanciful Nazi lampshade made from some Jew's skin. The guy replicated himself with his own skin —to do the same job he did during his life. Who the hell does such a thing? And how do you take your own skin off, tan it, and stitch it onto a dummy?"

Nash laid her hand over the vibrating, strained fist. "Easy girl. Inside voice, please. There are other people in other booths who are on the edge of remembering it's not a cat."

Muna frowned, and then her face exploded in a mix of horror and amusement. "Oh. That was a horrible meme." She looked at Celeste.

The woman's eyes rolled to one side in feigned boredom. "The fortune cookie said it wasn't chicken. Yeah, I've seen it. I didn't eat Chinese food for almost a day or two. Hollywood has a quirkier or worse sense of humor than most people. But yes, a little more sense of decorum."

Nash drew back her hand. "But the skin…?"

"That would include Bet Dorfman and her father. They owned the oldest and largest taxidermy company on the West Coast. If a big game hunter in the twenties to the fifties killed an elephant and wanted to display his trophy in his front room, he sent it home to Dorfman's. If you built your career on the back of a horse and were building a museum…"

Nash smirked. "You sent it to Dorfman. Along with your dog."

Celeste slow blinked. "You get the picture." She sipped a bit of the now lukewarm tea. "After the war, Valentine became a bit-part actor. Mostly a face in the crowd or a ranch hand or cattle puncher. Any work to pay the rent. Occasionally, he even got thrown a line or two. Nothing big. Certainly, no break-out part to turn into a career maker. But it paid the bills and a little more to stick away for a rainy day."

Muna blinked a few times. "But tanning your own…?"

Celeste held up her palm. "I'll get there. Trust me."

Powder adjusted on the chair and pushed her front paws a few times.

Nash stretched. "The little bladder needs a walk. But don't continue the story until I get back."

Celeste stood. "How about I continue the story in my backyard around the fire pit? It's… um… more private."

"If there's some scotch involved, I'm in."

"I believe there is a bottle of thirty-five-year-old private reserve."

Nash ballooned her left eye to enormous. "And you didn't lead with that?"

Celeste chuckled. "Not everyone drinks scotch. Personally, I'm more ready for some absinthe-laced green tea." She turned on Muna. "The tea is halal if I stop at just tea."

"Works for me. At this hour, I'm the driver, anyway."

27

VALENTINE

THE SMALL BACKYARD, after the dark grass, stretched for thirty miles across the sparkling sea of the San Fernando Valley. According to Celeste, brighter and more generous lighting made the larger streets and highways more visible. She had pointed and named each of the greater boulevards, Laurel Canyon, Coldwater Canyon, Van Nuys, and Ventura Boulevards.

The dark eyes of Muna and Nash mirrored the dancing flame of the fire pit as the logs turned to red lava and then crumbled into embers below.

"Growing up, we never had a fire in the backyard. The only time there was a fire was at funerals. The tribe and friends would gather around a bonfire and tell stories of the deceased."

Celeste hugged the large mug of tea to her chest. "Who do you remember most?"

Nash looked at the floating embers as they rose and then winked out in the air. "My parents. My father worked for the railroads. He always wore patched denim bib overalls. Stuffed deer heads and a few fish with corny notations on the plaques lined the walls of our living room. Things like grand champion thirty-four-pound trout caught on a twenty-eight-pound lure. Then, in parentheses, the punch line of the lure was still in the fish. It was an eight-pound sturgeon someone brought him and left in the bed of his truck. By the end of his shift, the un-gutted fish had ballooned like a beach ball. So he stuffed it that way."

"But the deer heads?"

Nash snorted. "Roadkill. We ate the jerky if the kill was still warm and not crawling with lice. But Dad had a book on taxidermy and was up to the challenge. He also made side money, stuffing a few things for other people. But the test pieces were on his walls. I studied at the kitchen table and ignored the painted marbles or ball bearings staring down at us. I guess my sister didn't want to touch them either."

"So you understand taxidermy."

"Intimately."

Celeste sipped on her tea as she studied the glazed, fixed stare of Muna's eyes. "What about your mother?"

Nash sipped on her tea as her left hand found the large curl of fur on the next chair. The nose was just past the edge of the seat, but the eyes closed. A soft moan rewarded her with a slow scratch on the tummy. "My mother, the enigma. A figure of duality. A nurturing parent but also a shaman who glimpsed into the future. As a child, I had my own prophetic visions, but I didn't want to be like her and inherit her gifts—or burdens, depending on your view."

"But you did."

Nash rocked gently. "A friend recently pointed out to me I already was as a little girl. I just didn't want to see that for myself. They were both powerful shamans, and it was my inheritance."

"And your sister?"

Nash shook her head. "It's like I got it all. But thankfully, where I drive, I never see roadkill. I think if I did, I'd have a strong over-powering urge to go check if it were still warm enough to butcher there on the side of the Washington Beltway." She looked up at the blond. "And you?"

Celeste snorted softly. "I grew up two blocks outside where the swells lived in Boston. Just close enough, so my parents struggled to keep up with the Shaws and Winthrops. Both teachers, they knew they weren't even close to the Cabots and Lodges, but they would kill themselves to appear above their stations in life. So until I ran as far away as possible, I had better memories of my many nannies and my father—a serial philanderer. Mother suffered from dipsomania and what we now call bipolar. She was manic at teaching and depressed when she got home to her nip of sherry. So I was ready for any crazy Hollywood could ever throw my way." Her head rolled over to Muna.

Nash snorted. "Muna fell into the fire long ago. I don't think she's ever seen a fire. Muna?"

The small face roused. And then blinked a few times. "Yes?" The voice was distant.

Celeste smiled. "We were talking about fires. Bonfires, camp-fires, or fireplaces… thoughts?"

She sipped on her mug and settled deeper into the canvas chair. "I've seen a few… on TV or movies on the computer. What was the question?" The voice sounded more like an eight-year-old than a mature woman.

"It wasn't important. But you wanted Valentine Diego. Before he became Eight Ball."

Muna struggled and sat more upright. "Yes, please."

"In the current entertainment industry, the ongoing joke is that every aspiring actor or actress ends up waiting tables. Unless you make it big, you'll always work side jobs. After Valentine returned from his military service, he found employment as a taxidermist working under Bet's father. Bet herself was a prime example of *taking your daughter to work*, as she contracted polio but fortunately walked with the aid of leg braces. It wasn't until her golden years when she also relied on a cane."

Muna pointed at the house. "The black one over the mantel?"

Celeste nodded. "That cane's the one she used at the Oscars. But her brown day-to-day is leaning next to the front door. So, from the sixth grade, when her mother died, her father homeschooled her at the taxidermy shop. She kept the stuffed animals clean, entertained the customers, and read every book she could get her hands on, which is where Valentine comes in. He was the tall, dark, and dashing young man who treated the little girl like she was an adult or at least a revered little sister."

Nash moved her vision from looking at the lights of the valley to Celeste standing over the small stack of firewood. "So a summer fall…"

Celeste vibrated her head. "Sibling only." She grabbed another log and placed it on the low fire. "There was a lot of fondness there but no romance. No. Valentine worked for her father if he didn't have a gig. And sometimes, you have a gig, but filming is at night, so you work during the day. But in the nineteen fifties, not so much. Especially with filming Westerns out in the wide-open deserts."

Muna rumbled in her slump. "Like the Alabama Hills in the Owens Valley."

Celeste's face lit up. "So you've been there."

"Close. We were in Big Pine a while back. I did some research on the area, which led to some clips on YouTube, which led to more time with Google Earth. But I recognized the rock he fell from."

"Back in the day, people referred to it as Dead Indian Rock." She held up her hand toward Nash. "Sorry. Different times."

"It's okay. We used to call them stupid white guy movies. But…" She shrugged. "… times change."

Celeste sat with a chuckle. "Touché." She picked up her mug and scowled at the empty bottom. "Well… so Valentine learned the movie industry and took a fall. From Dorfman, he learned the art of tanning and leaving the hair or fur on, and from Hollywood, he learned about bones and how the human body moves."

Muna held out her arms. "But your own…?"

"You're getting ahead of the story. But yes, it is the most macabre concept of anything Hollywood could produce. But it didn't start there. It started with him watching the daily rushes of a three-story fall he took into one of the first airbags. And then of a prop dummy dropping and hitting the car. And… as the story went, it bounced off without a dent. So they packed the dummy with bags of cold shot." She held up her finger and thumb with a tiny space between them. "It's a lead ball like a bee-bee. They use them in shotguns."

Muna chuckled as she looked at Nash. "Yeah, we don't know nothing about shotgun blasts." Both rolled their eyes.

Nash cleared her throat. "Powder and I caught the working end of the first serious case Muna worked as a field agent. And the first time she's saved my life."

The sound was small. "Oh."

Nash rocked with a smile and pointed at Muna. "Shot, blown up, shot again, pistol-whipped… Her mother thinks she ought to stop going out with me."

Muna jiggled with laughter. "Except I don't tell the parental units about any of the dangerous stuff. They're convinced I'm just a computer squint."

Nash zipped her mouth shut.

Celeste bobbed her head. "Smart move. But Valentine wound up taking a class at Glendale City College to learn how the bones work. He figured out how to make a skeleton move like a human skeleton but would endure the abuse of Hollywood. Next came the joints. They needed to move but also be twisted into positions. I don't know what the wire is called, but they use it in the taxidermy, and florists also use it. You can bend it thousands of times, but it never breaks."

Muna yawned. "The boys at the lab want to cut up Eight Ball to find out what they X-rayed. But they've had a lot of fun posing him at my desk or sitting around the autopsy lab. I need to get back just to play mommy kibosh with the little boy's shenanigans."

Celeste frowned. "What happens to Eight Ball once you're finished with the case?"

Nash rumbled a throat clearing. "We stuff him back in the space suit and put him back where we found him. We cannot remove anything because it is on the Navajo reservation. It all must remain where it's found."

Celeste stared at the deadpan face until the tiny snicker eked out of Muna. "I call horseshit."

Both agents exploded into chuckles. "Welcome to the quandary of so many cases." Muna rolled her hand and finger out into the air. "We had… well… Nash had a case involving a skeleton found in the creek where she grew up. When the number of skeletons increased, she asked for me to be transferred to San Francisco to assist with sorting all the bones. Well, the last count was over twenty, but we only identified five or six. We returned those to the families, or in one case, to the tribe, for burial. But our problem now is we have a container full of skeletons. More than any politician's closet could hold, but what do we do with them?"

Celeste grimaced as she tipped her head. "Potter's field? Donate to a college? What did you do?"

"Container SFFO seven-nine-three-six-P as in Papa, four sixty-two. Federal cold storage on a ship parked in the Sacramento River."

"Well, Valentine didn't have that problem. In the late fifties, as he was working out the dummies, doctors diagnosed him with cancer. So he put together a plan. First, he built one dummy, and with help from friends, they filmed the dummy. I've seen the film. It's impressive. They threw the guy off a train at high speed. The camera filmed the entire gag from the train. Another camera was on a car traveling alongside the train. The body moved like a human being killed." She stoked the embers and then got up to grab another log.

Sitting down, she continued. "There were shots of three people waiting on a park bench. The other two get up, and the dummy falls over with a knife in his back. But the best gag... or the most impressive, was the dummy being tossed from the twentieth floor of a new high-rise being built in downtown Los Angeles. They had four cameras rolling. One was from down the block, and you can see everything from the twentieth floor to the car parked below. First, there's an airbag where the car will be. The airbag in those days was only good for maybe five stories or fifty feet with a light person. But they were dropping from two hundred feet. The dummy destroyed the bag. And that was before they strapped another two hundred pounds of weight belts under the clothes. And this is all on film. They pull out the bag and park a 1955 Chevy Bel Air under the drop." She held up her hand.

"Now, remember, in those days, there's no stuntman guild yet. That's another five or six years away. So this is all wild west shit. But they drop the dummy. In the one clip, you see it complete from window to car. Then they feed in the closer film of the body and how the arms and legs move like a human instead of a large rag doll. And finally, all together, with proper editing, the dummy comes out of the window, flails in the air, and..." She slaps her hands together. "Flattens the car. The net weight and acceleration of thirty-two feet per second per second brings the body up to over a ton."

Nash rolled her head to look at the face of the human-computer. "And the answer is...?"

Muna blinked. "I'd have to check it, but Eight Ball weighs a little more than a hundred pounds. If they added two hundred more, he would fall two hundred feet, with an estimated impact arrest of a combined one foot from the metal roof, seats, and metal frame. You have in the neighborhood of thirty-one tons at impact."

"Ouch."

Nash looked back at Celeste. "Who did he show this proposal film to?"

"The then head of Burbank Studios, Reggie Magnason."

"And they bought the dummies."

"No." Celest shook her head. "No. It was much more complicated than a simple purchase. The deal was for eight dummies.

They would deliver seven dummies in the spring, but the last one wouldn't be ready until after Christmas during the hiatus. However, the payment terms were excessive and complicated, so it was mostly a handshake agreement between old friends. When Valentine first started, Reggie was a new assistant producer growing up swiftly in the ranks. About the time he became an executive producer, his uncle died and left him with an exceptionally large estate. Enough to buy his way into the top of the studios and secure his position as long as he wanted it."

Muna nodded. "Secure enough to make any deal for the dummies."

"Yes. But it wasn't really about the dummies. But guaranteeing the security for Betty Dorfman after her father passed as well as Valentine. It also locked in his place in Hollywood history for those of us who really knew the truth concerning Eight Ball."

"You mentioned a Bet before..."

"Yeah, the day I met Betty, she decided to transform herself into Bet. She knew Valentine and Reggie Magnuson gambled everything for her, so she wanted to play it safe. She was a cheesy, clichéd force, but a fantastic big sister, nonetheless. I was a junior assistant producer in my sophomore year of production when Reggie took notice of me. He sent for me and asked if I wanted a guaranteed job for life outside the traditional studio structure. I must've given him a skeptical look because he laughed and assured me this wasn't a sexual offer. Instead, I would become the personal assistant to a woman who could do anything she pleased: props, productions, acting, or even crafts. Her choice, and I was just along for the ride." Her face twisted with disgust. "If it sounds too good to be true... then it's Hollywood. He also mentioned if matters didn't work out, I could come back at a higher level with no hard feelings."

Nash rocked back with a small snort. "How long did you work for Bet?"

Celeste shrugged with a wry grin. "About three days."

Muna winced. "Ouch. What happened?"

"Our driver was a wonderful young man named Stuart. Stuart Stevens. He was always at Bet's beck and call and, by virtue of the job, mine. It was a Sunday morning. Stu and I had shown up at Bet's house at the usual seven. Stu had stopped by the bakery for bagels, lox, and cream cheese. As we walked up the walkway, Bet opened the door in a dressing gown. With a hateful look, she demanded to know what we were doing there."

Muna shrunk her chin into her chest and nuzzled the body armor with her chin. "Rut roe."

Celeste laughed. "Neither one of us counted on Stuart. He slid past Bet with a simple comment as he held up the bag. I've got bagels. And then marched straight to the kitchen. By the time we got in there, he had found the serrated knife, sliced the bagels, and popped them into the toaster. I followed his lead and dove for the coffee and pot. And that's when Bet fired us."

"Fired you?"

"Yup. As she grabbed the eggs out of the refrigerator, she told us she had worked with family all her life, and she'd be damned if she was going to do anything else. So I wasn't her assistant but became her little sister. Stuart became Cousin Stu. And we stayed a family until two thousand six when she passed away. I lived upstairs until she passed. Then I bought this place."

Muna sat up. "What about this Reggie guy?"

"Oh god. He was old. He retired in the mid-seventies. But his guarantee with Bet and us stood. The checks never stopped; Bet chose what we did. We voted on it over some nice dinner on the studio's credit card, and we were off on whatever the new grand adventure was."

Nash looked over as Powder stood and looked at her.

"Um..." She looked at Celeste. "Where..."

The woman waved her hand. "Over there. Anywhere near the palm. It's where my Pixie used to poop. The gardener is used to it. He just pitches it down the hill. I own the first three acres of hillside."

They watched Powder saunter to the designated tree and do her business.

"You didn't have to tell her where?"

Nash held her hands to the top sides of her head. "She has those big ears for a reason. She was listening."

They continued to watch Powder make her way from bush to bush, sniffing.

Nash laughed. "If you find any drugs, they're legal here in California. Be a nice guest."

Muna turned back to Celeste. "What happened to the driver, Stu?"

"Stu retired after Bet died. His husband and he have a limousine service in Carmel."

Nash glanced at her watch. "So what exactly was the agreement with Eight Ball?"

"So, like I said, Eight Ball was the eighth set dummy. Valentine's final stages of cancer took him in late July, which is why they didn't deliver the last dummy until after Christmas. He swore Dorfman to carry out his wishes because it would secure Betty's future. I don't know who did the skinning, nor would I ever want to know. But I'm sure it wasn't Bet."

Pragmatically, Muna lined out the sequence in the air with her hand. "So Valentine dies, Dorfman tans the skin and stitches it to the last dummy. So how did Bet or Betty get to the movie industry?"

"Shortly after Valentine's death, Bet moved to the storybook home on Hollywood Way. The studio provided the home. Craft stocked her pantry, and she was always under Reggie's protective wing with an income for life. Valentine had trusted his remains to Reggie and the studio, and so their obligation was to look after her. She would have no more cares for the rest of her life."

Nash swallowed. "Wow. Quite a deal."

"I think the studio got the best of the deal. Bet was a powerhouse. She never grabbed the spotlight. She always worked just outside of view. But she studied hard and guided things to run better. She assumed the position of executive producer and supported uncertain deals. But with her firm hand on the helm, she always ensured the studio's investment."

Muna shifted and pulled on the top of her body armor. "So what happens now?"

The blonde chuffed a small chuckle. "Excellent question. You have Eight Ball and who he is. From what Nate told me, you have a spacesuit from Apollo. It wouldn't fit in with my décor, but sitting them up in the corner of the living room would certainly stir up a conversation or two during a party. But is there anything I'm missing for this case of yours?"

Nash rumbled. "The big guy at the presentation."

"Lurch? What about him?"

"He knew where and what the ghost town was. But we still don't know why Eight Ball, and why there."

Celeste leaned forward as she pulled out her phone. Checking the time, she pushed an icon.

"Alexa, track down who rented Eight Ball last and for what project? Also, while I think about it, we need to go back to the coffee we were using a couple of months ago. This stuff smells like formaldehyde. Thanks. I'll be a little late. I have an early morning rack time." She hung up and slipped the phone back into her pocket. "And to think we used to have to write things down and then remember where we stuck the note."

Muna blinked with wide eyes. "Your Alexa can do all that?"

"She'd damn well better. Her mother is an exec in postproduction. Alexa is a PA2 and moving as fast as I can push her. I need her at the assistant producer level as soon as she can get her hours. We have work to do before I retire."

Nash kneaded her hand into Powder's chest, feeling the low moans. "And one brief phone call gets the answers we've been looking for…"

Celeste held up her finger as her other hand put a small log on the glowing embers. "But did you know the right questions to ask back when you started this investigation? But it's not always what you know, but who you know to ask. Alexa will find out who, ask the right questions, and get the answers, and I'll have the synopsis on my desk. And knowing Alexa, it will sit on top of a shooting script with notation tabs sticking out where Eight Ball was in the shoot."

Muna stood with Nash and her mugs. "When can we call you tomorrow?" She glanced at her watch. "Later?"

"My physical therapist will probably stretch me past nine, and then I'll need some script time over breakfast. So, how does after noon sound? Just ask for Alexa. She can give you the information and tell you who to call if you need more."

Nash stood. "We really appreciate you spending all this time with us."

"Honey, time spent with others is the most valuable commodity in this industry. Everyone talks about buying access, but what they truly seek is this. Gathering around a warm fire at night, exchanging tales and anecdotes. These evenings become written works on paper. Those get transformed into films, where people gather around their modern campfires through their televisions or movie screens to listen to the stories. We may have evolved from Neanderthals huddled in caves, but at our core, we are still simply storytellers."

28

THAT'S A WRAP

"You're late."

Nash and Muna looked up at the blonde waitress.

The woman took in the bloodshot eyes. "Oh god. You two clubbed hard last night."

Nash blinked. The face was clear of nose and lip rings. Her black Goth hair now sparkled a perky blond. The girl could pass for a fresh scrubbed church girl. "What happened to the... um...?" Her finger waved around the waitress's face.

"The Comic Illustrator's convention is over. Your usual? Or are we on to brunch?"

Muna coughed in her fist. "Oh, hell no. I don't think I could look at another menu."

"Usuals it is." She spun on her heel and disappeared.

Nash frowned at Muna. "Clubbing?"

Muna choked in a giggle. "Comic Illustrator's convention?"

"Gothing at will?"

Muna hung one eyelid low as she ground her head back and forth. "We need to go home. I can only take so much of this: eat, experience strange things, and eat more."

"I would have taken a picture yesterday, but then Mina might get some whacky idea for a new wig and look."

Muna scowled at her phone. "No. We need to really get home." She turned the phone toward Nash.

Baby had tied the hem of her T-shirt into a knot, making a crop top. The micro-mini skirt bordered on degenerate. The whorish makeup obviously came from the cadaver makeup set and maybe some of Muna's acrylic paints. She had brushed out her twisties into obvious extensions. Eight Ball truly looked like a happy camper, with the little slut cuddled into the larger body.

"Oh goodness. Nobody is in charge."

The gigantic shadow paused for a moment. "Fire Tramp Lady cosplay. But who's the naked dude with the wonky eye?"

Muna turned the screen back and enlarged it. "Tramp?"

The waitress laid out their plates and bowls. "Lady and the Tramp? The Disney cartoon dog movie from like a century ago?"

Muna nodded as she picked up her mug. "Yeah, I get the cartoon movie... but cosplay?"

"Yeah. It was a massive thing at Comic-Con last year. It'll probably be down to the kids this year. How old is the chick?"

Nash growled. "Seventeen going on old enough to know better."

"Ouch for you mommy. Who's the creeper whose lap she's sitting in?"

Muna laughed and pointed at Nash. "Mommy?" She handed the phone to the waitress. "He's a set dummy."

She pinched and expanded the screen. "Dude. That's way better than doing a crash dummy. That's the best stage-down costume I've seen."

"No. It's not a costume. He's... It's a dummy for the movies. They dress them up and throw them off buildings and stuff. He's not naked... just... um... not dressed."

"His face looks real."

Muna held out her hand. "It's hard to explain."

She handed the phone back. "Set dummy. I wonder how I could do the body…"

Nash rolled her eyes. "Just do a blow-up sex doll."

"Nah. So, five years ago. Your jaw aches for days after holding the O-face for so long. And all the guys want to check if everything works. Not the best cosplay idea to come down the boulevard." She floated back into the restaurant.

"We really need to go home."

THE FREEWAY SLOWED WORSE THAN THE LAST TWO DAYS. Muna fed her phone through the speaker and the hand-free system in the SUV. "Hey, Chris, what's up in special effects land?"

"After you guys came out, I raked the dead coal records back before the plague. Street Fire Productions rented the Apollo Eleven suit. Don't even write it down. I looked them up for you. Production did the stunts for Wild West Cinema, a group out of Burbank Studios. Wild West got Street Fire their insurance and rental creds. Evidently, the head of Street Fire was one of the first people to get COVID-19 and was hospitalized and planted before they needed refrigerator trucks. Which is why the insurance paid us for the non-return on the rental."

Nash cleared the mirrors and signaled for the exit lane. "So this Street Fire is a dead end. How about the Wild West show?"

"We checked out some knives to them about six months ago. Nate at Burbank would be a good start for tracking them down and getting their story."

Muna snickered. "Boy Chris, you are like so two days ago on this. We moved up to Celeste Dumont level last night."

His laugh had a large echo. He was obviously in his warehouse area. "Oh, sure. Four days in Hollywood, and you pull out the Queen of Hearts card. But have you had Chinese dinner with her?"

Nash laughed. "Keep reaching chuckles. Try most of the night sitting around her fire pit."

"Well, you've reached the peak. I tried to get her to adopt me years ago. We set up some of her house. The fire pit looking over the valley is the best. So what more can I do for the FBI?"

Muna licked her lips. "When we bring Eight Ball, the dummy, back to Wicky at Universal… do you…?"

"The suit? Nope. It got paid for in full back in twenty-two. It would just confuse things. Do you have a use for it? Target practice? Pin the life support on the astronaut? Anything?"

Muna smiled large and toothy at Nash, shaking her head. "Yeah, I think we can find some room in the storage area. Thanks."

"No problem. I need to get back to fixing a rainmaker if there's nothing more."

"Nope. We're good. Thanks again for all your help and an amazing day at Global Effects."

Nash glanced over at Muna, giggling at the passenger window as they exited the frozen freeway. "You're shameless."

The smile reflected in the glass. "Yup." She ground her head back to face Nash. "I hope the suit fits."

"Hah. Neil Armstrong was my size. I looked him up."

Nash eased the black SUV into the driveway and up to the guard shack. She lowered the window.

"Were here to see Alexa… um…" She peered over at Muna. "Celeste never told us a last name." She looked back at the laughing guard. "What?"

He pointed to where they had parked the day before. "She's on her way down."

The cart stopped as Nash threaded the SUV into the parking slot.

The young woman dropped to her knees when she saw Powder. "Celeste promised I get to pet."

Powder glanced back, and Nash pointed.

Powder danced sideways at the girl's little girl voice for cute animals. The butt vibrated as she snuggled in for a hug and a pet.

Muna stopped. "Shit. Now I'm jealous. I never get the side dance."

Nash blustered her lips. "Fuck you. I never get the wiggle butt, either."

The redhead rolled her head sideways to look at the two agents. "I never get to pet dogs. My mother is seriously allergic. So I'll have to burn these clothes and go to the gym and steam before I go home. What's her name?"

"It's on her badge, but her name is Powder."

Alexa picked up the front two legs. "You have a badge? There's a... Look at you. An official badge-packing G-girl. How about a gun?" She peered at both sides. "Nope. I guess that's why you bring your posse."

Alexa stood and held out her hand. "Hi. I'm Alexa. Sorry for getting distracted. But... well... it's a dog."

Nash smirked. "We get it. You have some information for us?"

"Yeah. Climb in. I laid it out on the office conference table."

The short drive contained a few turns. The last turn drove through a giant open door. They glided to the end of the sound stage. "Welcome to home sweet home... for the month." She turned the cart and stopped in front of several large tables. "We're on this one."

Nash snorted as she scanned around the cavernous building. Leaning close to Muna, she snickered. "Got space envy yet?"

"No. And the term is cave coveting. You people have a commandment about it. But there's no such directive in the Quran. We just live and enjoy."

Alexa glanced up at the two women looking around. "Oh. Yeah. It's not the biggest they've stuck us in, but it beats trying to get things done on a shooting set. We were in the kitchen of one set while they shot film in the living room. Only the dining room separated us." She turned to the stack of documents on the table. As she peeled each document, she explained. "This is the general ledger for Space Cowboy." She glanced up. "Oh. Yeah. Your set had a working title."

Nash vibrated her head. "We didn't know."

"I'd go through the names, but most are probably meaningless to you. But Eight Ball... is... this one. Wild West Cinema... well, back then. Now they are Wild West Productions. But I heard a rumor they have taken out copyrights and sales marks to register West Stream Systems or something. When it happens, we'll hear about it. So here's their prospectus, glory rag, so you can learn if you want to get in bed with them, and their financials."

Muna leaned in. "We don't need financials."

"The financials are bullshit. This is all the stuff they take to the bank to get better loans if they can't find a factor." She peered up at the blank faces. "Investors. Backers? Money people? Mom and Dad? Rich uncle? GoFundMe?"

Nash chuckled. "We get it."

Muna spread some files. "So Wild West Cinema rented Eight Ball. But Street Fire rented the spacesuit? Why wouldn't Street Fire just rent both?"

Alexa slumped back onto her right hip as she studied the two faces. "Okay, here's the nickel college class on how Hollywood works." She pointed at Muna. "You have fifty cents. And she has fifty cents. The rent on Eight Ball is thirty-five cents, and the rent on the spacesuit is twenty-five." She stood waiting.

Nash smirked. "So I'll rent one, and Muna rents the other."

"Right. But the way it really works is, what does your insurance cover? Set dummy goes under incidentals. But a spacesuit goes under props."

Muna frowned. "Why not costumes?"

"Because the space suit can get plugged in."

"Plugged into what?"

The blonde shrugged. "Electricity, heater, air, water... anything you can plug into the suit. But what do you plug your shirt into? Nothing. That's a costume. It also comes down to who touches the item—props or costumers. Set dressers or seamstresses."

Muna bounced her eyebrows. "Huh."

Nash growled. "It sounds complicated."

Alexa straightened. "Multi-layered, but also straightforward once you get the hang of it." She slumped on her right hip. "Let's say you're shooting a shoot-out. You only have two actors. But you also have a few cameramen and assistants. The list includes the director, assistant director, production assistant, and makeup artist for each actor, writer, lighting director, and their assistants. You get the idea. All told, you might have thirty to fifty people standing in the street you'll never see in the movie. But each person has their place. And each person in a union ensures they know what they're doing at whatever level they're hired at."

Muna laid her finger on the stack of files. "Armorer. The weapons expert."

The young woman rocked with her understanding of the real question. "It was a non-union-sanctioned set. Everyone worked scab. It happens. A union armorer would have had many years of experience working alone and would never allow live rounds on the set. They would have cleared the gun with no bullets in a cold gun. On a union set, it would have never happened. In my humble opinion, which I would never attest to in court. Or I'd be looking for a new job in Canada as a dog walker." She glanced over at Powder. "Newcomers enter the industry at the bottom rung as lowly production assistants. These eager beavers dedicate endless hours doing the most menial of the scut work. Yet, they unknowingly absorb knowledge about every aspect of the job and industry. With experience, they climb the ranks to Second-Second, Assistant Director level two, and finally AD-1, but their responsibilities still include running errands for others. Only those others are the cream, like Executive Producers and Directors. So eventually, they're here…" She chopped her hands at her hips. "… on the cusp of becoming someone. I'm enormously lucky Celeste found me and took me under her wing. During my first year, she gave me tons of books and stuff to read in all my spare time. I survived on three hours' sleep and whatever food I could snatch off a Craft's table. But I survived. And I know the person above me knows we both did the work. There are no shortcuts. I know Celeste told you about her old boss, Bet. But Bet was never in the system. She was the unicorn. But she earned everyone's respect because of how she worked. For her, there was work and nothing else. Nobody can or wants to aspire to that. We want to have dinner with a friend or sleep in late on Sundays—we want a life."

Nash studied Muna. Muna twitched and glowered at Nash. "I hear her. I'm working on getting a life."

Alexa sensed something going on, not concerning her or the investigation. She spread the rest of the stack. "Here's everything else I could pull up about the project. But basically, Covid hit and shut down everything. Several people died, and the industry moved on. We worked around learning how to shoot differently. More shooting in remote locations, or at least in the open air. I printed a shooting script for you and inserted markers indicating where Eight Ball and the spacesuit got used." She re-stacked the pile. "If you can't fit these in your suitcases, I can ship wherever you want."

Muna vibrated her head. "Nah, I'll make it work. I'll fit every-thing in the spacesuit helmet, and any extra can go in my roll-on."

Nash stuck her hand out. "You and Celeste have been amazing. This will wrap up the investigation nicely."

Alexa smiled. "I could tell by Celeste's tone this morning; she was as thrilled as I was to work on this. We make stories every day. Every bit of made-up fantasy. But this was a real-life mystery, and it involved us. It's the stuff we can tell future generations stories about."

Muna smirked. "Around campfires."

Alexa breathed a single, airy laugh. "At least a fire pit."

As the blonde dropped them at the SUV, she grew shy. "Do you have the helmet with you now?"

Muna laughed. The two were geek twins under the skin. One for science, the other for movie making. "You can even try on the gloves."

The geek's face lit up. "Wow."

29

HEADING HOME, MAYBE

THE HARRIED WOMAN in the rumpled uniform walked past. "Just leave the keys on the dashboard. We'll email you a receipt."

Nash stepped two back-steps away from the SUV. "HEY!" Her bark was unapologetically Marine Lieutenant.

The woman's shoulders flinched as she stopped and turned on one heel and the other toe. Her turn didn't have any snap left, but Nash recognized the long-forgotten response. She took two steps back toward Nash and stopped. They were on her turf.

Nash quietly walked to the obviously harried rental car woman. Nash had only counted to five, but it was enough. Her voice was calm. "Sorry for the bark. It's been a long day. Probably not as long or as hard as yours, but more than I'm used to. But I need you to go over our unit and check it in. We get a lot of crap about turning in vehicles with bullet holes and dead bodies in the truck. It goes with our job, but it's tiresome. We need you to make sure nobody scratched the paint or loaded the wrong fuel." She handed out the small white receipt. "We topped it off a klick down the street."

The Latina, a decade older than Nash, studied the receipt as her eye also took in the badge on the belt. She scratched at the short, curly haircut. "Which branch?"

"Marines."

The woman scanned the ID on the key. "Yeah, Dad was a lifer. They cut the threads deep into his head. I was close. Six years on the Lexington was enough." She turned to the SUV as Muna closed the back doors. She pointed at Powder. "I wish I'd done K-9s. How did the pig drive?"

Nash looked at Muna, following them around the SUV.

"Slow response in the throttle. It is not a hesitation, but it is not snappy like it should be. And when you brake in traffic, she wants to pull to the left slightly. Besides that, she's great for mom and the soccer kids but drifts like a bloated whale in the deep sand. I'd give it two and a half stars."

The woman barely glanced back. She pointed at the side above the right front tire. "You scratched the quarter-panel." Rubbing it, she then licked her thumb. "Nope. My bad—just bird shit." She looked at Muna. "Any dead bodies in the back?"

Muna pointed at the large padded black bags. "Nah, we cut them up, and we're taking the pieces with us. It's one of those no-frills flights. Not even peanuts. I'm active, and I get hungry."

The woman finally eked out a tired smile as she walked past Nash. "You three have a fantastic flight. I'll make a note about you detailing the unit before returning."

"Thanks."

As Muna checked in the extra bags, Nash studied her phone and then slid it back into her pocket.

Muna pointed at the counter. Nash shook her head. "I'm on American, but it just got delayed by four hours. I guess I'll go find dinner for Wiggles and me."

"Okay. I still need to go deal with TSA. I'll check with you tomorrow."

Nash twitched her chin out. "What about Eight Ball?"

"I have a little time coming. I was thinking about driving him down. If he's sitting shotgun, I can ride the HOV lanes…"

Nash shook and hung her head. "Three days in Hollywood, and you're already becoming a criminal."

Muna chuckled. "I won't need to. I'll bring the urban assault unit with all the fancy signage. Anyway, I figured I'd go on down and get my toenails painted for a couple of days. Check in with the family. Next month is still in the air, but it could become busy."

Nash frowned and then blinked her face clear. "Oh yeah. Keep me posted if you get on the team. And have a nice flight."

Muna pointed at Powder, pumping her front paws. "Yeah, you need to go take a walk."

Nash and Powder watched as Muna took the turn to TSA for flight crews and law enforcement. Nash returned the last wave. Pulling her phone out of her pocket, she returned the text.

"We'll meet you out front of Alaska."

The thumbs-up emoji was instantaneous.

Jazz was standing by the door of the gray SUV. The Deep Six dredge logo filled the door panel.

Nash pointed at Powder. Jazz pointed back the other way, and Nash saw the dog symbol.

"It's why we parked here."

As Powder finished. The stretched SUV eased up along the curb. The side door rolled back.

As Powder jumped in and up onto the center console, Ming hugged her and laughed back at Nash. "Welcome to the Lesbian Limo Service."

Nash chuckled. "So, care to explain the clandestine message and the canceling of my flight?"

Jazz turned in the passenger seat as Nash buckled her belt. "One, we thought you'd like more legroom. And two, we have better food and scotch."

Ming turned right down a side street, running alongside the freeway. "We can always drop you back, and you can cram into a stinky seven-thirty-seven and eat rubber chicken. Or you can sip on better scotch and dine on Chateaubriand with baby veggies taken before their prime. I think the dessert will be some stinky old flan or something else horrid."

Nash rolled her eyes. "And the airplane is...?"

"A new Gulfstream. We have business in D.C., and we need to talk to you, Mina, and your guardian."

"What about?"

"Next month."

Nash noted the turn into another airport and the lack of crowds. Ming nosed the SUV up to an enormous hangar.

"I thought next month is still up in the air?"

Ming's door cracked. "Some parts. But not everything."

MUNA SHUFFLED THROUGH THE OFFICE AREA. THE Minions, making up each slipper, stared up at the Hello Kitty pajamas under the World War Two Navy flak vest. She stopped at her desk. The dummy sat holding out her Captain America coffee hydro flask. She took the flask and realized the weight. Opening the lid, she smiled at the aroma.

"The Pew-Pew Master called and told us you got home. He said you'd need coffee because you were... and I'm quoting him here... running a triple bag of hurt."

Muna chuckled as she looked over at Baby standing with Chips. "Pew-Pew Master? I'm never going to think of Lester any other way now."

Chips raised a single eyebrow. "Before you explain the Minions slippers, I want to know what a triple bag of hurt is."

Muna closed her eyes and thought while she sipped on the coffee. "Oh god... I needed this." She looked at Chips. "Are you two leaving today?"

The blond ponytail vibrated as she pointed at the double empire, which had grown larger in the corner. "Don't have to. But... well, we're kind of missing Chef's cooking."

"How about giving me an hour to take a shower and make some arrangements? Better yet, find where I can buy a heavy-duty shipping box for Eight Ball here. I need to send him home to Hollywood."

"One-way?"

"No. The boys get one of the really beat-up sibling dummies to do whatever they want with—including cutting him open and doing an autopsy."

Baby hung her head and side-eyed Muna. "What about the spacesuit?"

"Why?"

Chips snickered. "Oz wouldn't fit, and Mike is too stuffy to try..."

Muna fished the air with her hand. "Show me the other pictures. And by the way, a waitress in Santa Monica thinks your Lady and the Tramp outfit was on fire."

Baby rolled her eyes. "It's just fire. The word on would be something the Boomers would say."

Chips tapped on Muna's computer screen. The tiny, animated avatar of Baby was doing jumping jacks.

Muna clicked and immediately wished she hadn't. The hot coffee burned her nose as it shot out onto the keyboard. "I'm taking a shower. I need a new keyboard."

THE FUNERAL HOME DIDN'T UNDERSTAND, BUT FOUR hundred dollars is four hundred dollars.

Baby rested her arm on the plywood casket as they drove away. "The cardboard one was a lot cheaper. I'm just sayin'."

Muna glanced back. They folded down the larger half of the split seat to accommodate the casket. Baby sat in the other third of the seat. "James said the cardboard casket isn't FAA certified. But the plywood one is."

"But there was one with just the box without the pillow and fabric stuff. It was only three hundred."

Muna cleared the next lane and flicked the blinker. "What, and have Eight Ball's last journey be bare bones? Just pack the dummy like a used rag doll. Rattle the dummy in a box? Pack the dummy like last year's trash? They box children's trash computers with more respect. Mice even get a form-fitting blister pack."

Baby ran her fingers along the smooth edges of the former display model wooden box. The glossy finish reflected the tinted windows. She sighed, her voice carrying a hint of sadness. "I suppose it wasn't meant to last. But he was a fun distraction for a while."

Chips snorted. "You have five thousand photos to remember your first date forever." She turned around and looked out the window as Muna charged the SUV up the on-ramp. "Where to now?"

Muna glanced over with a smirk. "We were in Southern California. I could smell the food; except we had everything *but* great burritos."

Chips smiled. "Pablo burritos, it is."

"I'm home, Baby."

The small black girl leaned forward from the second seat. "What?"

<hr>

THE AFTERNOON HEAT ROASTED THE RIFLE RANGE. THE three stood with their earmuffs up on their heads. Muna handed Baby two pairs of surgical gloves. "Put these on first."

"There's four here."

"Both pair." She looked at Chips. "Which pistol do you want to try?"

"Which one is the triple bag of hurt?"

Muna pointed at the Smith & Wesson 500. "You'll get all the kick you can handle and then some. The first shot will give you some sense of what it feels like to be blown up."

"Ouch. What about the other one?"

"The Desert Eagle is the same caliber, but it reduces the kick by channeling the gas into the slide. So he'll push you around but still respect you the next morning."

"I'll try the nicer one."

Baby held up her blue hands. "Okay. Now what?"

Muna closed her eyes. "Take the two off your... which hand do you shoot with?"

"Left."

"Take the gloves off your right hand and pull them onto your left, so you have all four gloves on your left hand. Then, put the leather glove on, but stand over here and pull your earmuffs down. Chips is going to dance with the demon." She turned back to Chips.

Chips showed her the leather glove was tight. "Okay, I slide the... um... clip. I slide the clip into the handle and then hit it with my left palm until it clicks. Then I pull back the slide and let it snap back. That means it's loaded and cocked."

"And always point the end of the gun out there. At the target. Okay. Do it slow."

Chips loaded the gun and pulled the slide.

"All the way until it stops. Then let it go."

The slide snapped back.

Muna pulled the woman's earmuffs down from behind and then patted her on the back. "You don't have to aim. Just think about squeezing an overripe gra—"

The gun boomed. Baby jumped, but Chips stood frozen. "Did I hit the target?"

Muna thought about the small kick of dirt halfway up the sand hill behind the target. "You hit exactly where I told you to aim. How do you feel? Want to take another hit?"

"Um… sure. Baby, take a picture for Slug."

"On it."

Muna chuckled. This was going to take longer than she had thought.

30

A GOOD DAY TO ENJOY SAN FRANCISCO WEATHER

THE CHILLY DRIZZLE broke into a little sprinkle. Rolled towels lay just inside the thresholds of the doors. The thin plastic ponchos hung in hues of red, white, and blue. The colors waved, collected, and parted again as the people stepped outside or walked out of the rooms and wandered the halls of the two floors of the hotel.

Jazz leaned with her back to the jamb of the French doors opened to the small veranda and the view of the Seine. Jazz had dyed her spiked hair to resemble an American flag. The fingers running through the stripes had matching nails. The Latina leaned her head into Jazz's shoulder. "I'm glad the commander gave me the time off."

Jazz turned her head and kissed the top of the black hair. "You don't mind the rain?"

"With you, I prefer being drenched by the rain in this romantic city than standing watch for another sunny day in Newport. I get three hundred and fifty-three days of sunshine and heat every year. But Olympics or no Olympics, I'll come here with you any day." She pointed at the jet ski on the river. "Is this the start? Or just flashing us?"

Jazz laughed at the blue strobing light on the front of the jet ski.

She glanced into the large room and whistled sharply. "Hey, guys. The first cop's coming down the river. Spread the word."

Ming whipped out her cell phone, and her thumbs blurred on the keyboard. The phone erupted in the sound of a klaxon horn. Tree laughed as she hip-checked her partner. "Girl. You're slowing down in your old age."

Felix leaned around Tree and showed Ming his cell phone. The view was of the river and active. "I stuck a minicamera out there on the veranda. It beats standing out there and watching. The fun girl is in here." His left arm squeezed Tree's waist.

In the next room, Nash checked her phone and then turned back to the older couple. "They said the parade is coming. Let me help you with your poncho."

Mrs. al-Faragi patted Nash's hand. "In Pittsburg, we call this kind of weather liquid sunshine. This wouldn't even water the lawn. We didn't come all the way to Paris just to hide away from whatever the sky wants to give us." She gripped the hand. "As long as it isn't eight feet of snow in six hours. Those days are not the kindest."

Nash looked at the gentleman in the matching windbreaker of stars and stripes. She shrugged her head and eyes at the veranda doors. "Did you two get enough to eat? Was everything okay?"

Mr. al-Faragi beamed. "The man they call Chef said everything is halal. So, who am I to ask what we're eating? But maybe a few of the recipes would be nice to learn. Other than that, this has been a magical vacation."

They stepped out onto the veranda. As they looked back along the top floor of the hotel overlooking the Seine, the women of Deep Six filled every veranda. Some were waving small American flags, others simply soaking in the experience.

Mina and Lele stepped out behind them and looked along the collective verandas. "Where are the boys?"

Nash snickered as she pointed at the floor of the veranda. "The boys have the fourth floor. The older ones have the matching corner suites like this one, and the younger kids have the dormitory pajama parties." She leaned to scratch Powder's head and found a hand already there. Nash smiled at Mrs. al-Faragi. The woman shrugged.

"We'll be next door with the beignets and chocolate." Mina and Lele waved over their heads. Their two ponchos made a complete American flag.

Netti and Nash scratched the dog's head. "In our culture, dogs are rare." She shrugged again. "Now I know why Muna loves this dog. And she feels good to pet." She looked up. "It's Netti, by the way. Netti and Armand. Some call him Ari, but that's a personal choice."

"Nash. We're all family. And I'm glad you're here to support her."

Netti pointed at the wall separating the next suite of rooms. "We met Jazz and her Maria at the shoot in Dallas. We had asked at the hotel information desk if there were any Ethiopian restaurants nearby. The concierge pointed at the two women and said they were getting a shuttle to the restaurant. So we joined them. Jazz said she wanted to learn about the food a good friend grew up on. There aren't many Munas in America. So the cat was loose. Then, we ran into them at the Colorado shooting meet. It was kismet."

Nash frowned. "How long have you been following your daughter's shooting?"

"Ari heard from a friend about a year ago. The man said there was an FBI agent who made an impression at a local competition there in Florida. He wanted to know if we had heard of a Muna al-Faragi. Ari pleaded innocence and asked if he had a link to any articles. It's not a common name—especially in the American shooting world."

Nash chuckled. "And combine it with the FBI... you only end up with one person. But you're okay with her shooting?"

Netti straightened as she laughed. She grabbed at her husband's arm. As he turned, she giggled. "Nash wants to know if we are okay with Muna shooting. I guess because of our pacifist beliefs."

He scowled and slowly shook his head. "Have you tasted the snacks she's addicted to?"

"You knew about the hot rinds?"

Netti laughed. "I used to find the bags buried in her closet when she was in high school. Ari and I talked. Every day, we see children and drugs. Where is the harm in something so hot it burns the halal out of it? Yes, I used that pun. But where's the harm? Kids get in trouble with their computers these days. Look where computers took her." She wound her finger in her long curls. "We used to wear hijabs. Now, only a few at our mosque still adhere. When I was a little girl in Tehran, women wore short skirts, sleeveless blouses, and a scarf if it matched the outfit. Or not. Now... Tehran is trying to go back to the eleven hundreds and burqas. We can be pacifists and still support a daughter we love—who shoots guns—and eats pork rinds. It hurts no one—except criminals. Yes?"

Nash rocked her head gently. "But you need to sit down and talk about all of this with her. Trust me. Her... um... inner self needs some calm in there. How much do you know of her job?"

Ari turned and leaned in. "What is the term she uses for the computer work? Squirt?"

"Squint. Because computer people squint or narrow their eyes when they look at bad computer monitors."

"When we came out to San Francisco, we saw her computer. Well... wall of computers." He held his spread right hand to block the air. "The two monitors on the right of her desk were turned off. She said they needed work. I don't think she's the type of person to tolerate a broken computer. It's what she's afraid to show her parents, who might worry. But we also noticed the body armor she always wears—I suspect even here. Nobody thinks to wear so much weight on a whim—especially if you sit at a computer all day. I didn't put on mine until the Pittsburg Transit made me. Do we worry about her? Certainly, she's at the front and finish of our daily prayers. But she is our daughter. But she is also a… how do they say it these days? A grown-assed woman?"

Nash chuckled. "That she is."

They could hear Jazz through the veranda doors. "Hey, guys. The opening ceremony is in view."

Netti held her palm out. "Shall we join the rest of the fan club on the veranda?"

RESEARCH BEYOND THE LIBRARY

Ask any professor or student, and they will tell you how research makes academia tick. Ask a librarian, and they can tell you it is the lifeblood of their business. Writers, on the other vein, will divulge how it is the juice thathand, will divulge how the juice makes blood runny enough to flow.

During a recent interview, **Baer Charlton, '82, Anthropology,** a mystery writer, chuckled at the idea of doing research in a library or on a university campus. "There are so many more interesting ways to become informed or gather an understanding."

Baer Charlton has relinquished many passports, circling the globe in his quest for creative fuel and enlightenment. He has wandered the arid deserts of America, listened to the symphony of a rainforest growing in Costa Rica, and witnessed the primal act of lions mating in Tanzania's Ngorongoro Crater. If he ever writes a story about how female mountain gorillas choose their next alpha male by urinating on them, it will be full of the vivid memories his own back carries.

During his research on the Apollo Program's EVA suits, he had to become very familiar with the process of putting on the suit. With all the ins and outs of the complicated suits, it was no quick experience. And if you are going to research something science, it is advisable to have a geek friend as your wingman—or woman.

As NASA phased out the older suits, ships, and equipment, some found their way into the hands of collectors. Others became the research foundation for replication and use in the entertainment industry. When it comes to spacesuits for movies, Global Effects Labs in Sylmar, CA, is the top supplier.

Charlton reached out to Christopher Gilman, owner of Global Effects, and proposed a passion project. (Euphemism for No Pay.) Charlton explained the depth he needed to understand about the critical details making up the unique suits. Especially the workings and mechanics of the seal rings on the boots, gloves, and helmets— as it was a critical detail in his upcoming book.

The initial foray into the details ran longer than a seminar. Leaving no time for in-depth insertion into the suit. Establishing a second meeting meant also meant setting another goal—one for education. With the goal of putting on the suit, and verbal explanation of the complexities, filming would be required. Requiring a second, or in this case, a third person, to film the process. For that, one needs to find the biggest science nerd you know.

Charlton dialed the UCI Alumni Association and inquired if **Blake Stone, '05 BS**, could use his phone and take pictures while wearing an orange **ACES** space suit. (**Advanced Crew Escape Suit** —from the Shuttle Program)

There may or may not have been some fangirl squealing involved in the reply.

Astronauts used the white **Extra Vehicular Activities (EVA)** suit during the lunar landings during the Apollo program. The sixty-pound spacesuit is actually three layers of suits. The inner is the pressure suit. A The middle contains all the electronics and life support. The light/heat reflective outer shell is the tough skin to that protects everything inside. A fourth layer is called the diaper shell and gets inserted into the suit before it's put on. It traps the sweat and any other liquids from contaminating the spacesuit.

There aren't any dry cleaners in space. However, astronauts can roll up the thin diaper shell to the size of a cigar and stow it for disposal back on Earth.

The resulting video, which should be searchable on YouTube, explains how to put the suits on.

On Earth, astronauts put on suits while sitting down. The legs are first. The dresser (extra person) is critical to make sure the astronaut's feet don't get lost. And then they guide the feet through the unforgiving ankle rings.

Once both legs are in the suit, you bring the suit's waist up to the thighs. Then, the best description of the next move is to "dive into the suit". ." The arms go into the sleeves as the head ducks and aims for the ring. The neck ring is roomy, and once the head is out, the astronaut can swim his arms toward the wrist rings. (Which are not so roomy.)

Once the feet, hands, and head are out, the astronaut shimmies their shoulders into the suit and then stands up. The standing draws the body and backside into the suit, and voila—you're good for takeoff. Okay,... it's good to zip up the back and put on the large, oversized boots. (The boots are large because of the astronaut's giant feats.) Actually, they have the astronaut's shoes strapped inside the boots so the boots don't slop around but can still be pressurized.

Astronauts wore the orange ACES suit during takeoff and landings of the shuttleshuttle landings. The orange color would make them easy to spot in case of a crash landing. But However, after the Columbia blew up, the more comfortable blue flight suits replaced the ACES.

ALSO BY BAER CHARLTON

The Very Littlest Dragon: NEW Editions
(All-new full-color ebook, a paperback with
coloring pages, and a full-color Collector's Edition hardback)

Stoneheart — Pulitzer Nominee 2015
Angel Flights
What About Marsha?
Pirate's Patch
Flat Surf

I Drink Coffee and Make Shit Up
One Writer's Journey Without Signposts

JOLIE "ROCKET" ROBERTS SERIES
Dry Bridge of Vengeance – Book One
Dry Ridge of Redemption – Book Two

THORNY WALLACE SERIES
Death in the Valley – Book One
Light to Light – Book Two

SOUTHSIDE HOOKER SERIES
Death on a Dime – Book One
Night Vision – Book Two
Unbidden Garden – Book Three
Boomtown – Book Four
One Day Under the Grass – Book Five
Southside Hooker Series: Books 1–5 Box Set
(Collector's Edition hardback & ebook available)

<u>Nash Running Bear Mysteries</u>
A Skeleton in Bone Creek – Book One
Double-time Out of Taos – Book Two
Three Crows East of Empty – Book Three
Four-corner Spread – Book Four
Cinco D' Mojave – Book Five
Six-sided Crap Shoot – Book Six
Seven Grams of Vengence – Book Seven
Eight Ball in the Sand Trap – Book Eight

<u>Nash Running Bear Shorts</u>
Shrinkage

ABOUT THE AUTHOR

Bestselling author Baer Charlton graduated from UC Irvine with a degree in Social Anthropology, monkeyed around for a while, and then proceeded onward with a life of global travel, multi-disciplinary adventure, and meeting the memorable array of characters he would come to describe in his writing. He has ridden things with gears, engines, and sails, and made things with wood, leather, and metal. He has been stitched back together more times than the average hockey team; his long-suffering wife and an assortment of cats and dogs have nursed him back to health after each surgery.

Baer knows a lot about many things in this world. History flows through his veins and pours out of him at the slightest provocation. Do not ask him what you may think is a simple question unless you have the time to hear a fascinating story.

You can find more at
www.mordantmedia.com